PRINCESS AND THE PIRATE

Matching Galaxies 1

F.L. Journey

Paperback ISBN-13: 978-1-965176-12-2

Ebook ISBN: 978-1-965176-11-5

For information, please contact publisher at faireydragonpress@gmail.com

Table of Contents

CHAPTER 1..1

CHAPTER 2..7

CHAPTER 3..12

CHAPTER 4..16

CHAPTER 5..23

CHAPTER 6..32

CHAPTER 7..43

CHAPTER 8..50

CHAPTER 9..56

CHAPTER 10..71

CHAPTER 11..89

CHAPTER 12..98

CHAPTER 13..115

CHAPTER 14..136

CHAPTER 15..154

CHAPTER 16..170

CHAPTER 17..183

CHAPTER 18..192

CHAPTER 19..212

CHAPTER 20..230

About Author 233

Other books by Author..234

Dedication

To our ARC readers. Thank you so much for all the support.

We hope you're ready for the rollercoaster that is yet to come!

CHAPTER 1

The bodies around me were slick with sweat. With the music bumping, time flowed like a river. My silver skin reflected the lights flashing in rhythm with the music. The club's owners bringing in a Mars based EDM DJ was a great choice for my birthday. I didn't even have to ask them; they already knew, and what a birthday party it was. While everyone else was taking drugs, I was sober. It wasn't because I was the princess, I'd never thought getting high was for me. That didn't stop me from loving the clubbing experience. This was where I belonged, among the dancers without a care in the world.

I glanced over at my security guard, Roald. He was on the intercell, deep in conversation. This was unusual because his attention was usually on me. Being the princess and only child of the King of Io, the fourth largest and soley inhabited moon of Jupiter, I was special. Not thinking twice about it, I moved back to the group of Martians. Their red skin and black hair and eyes reflected the DJ's lights. As I got closer to the DJ, I lost myself to the music. At least I was, until someone grabbed my arm. I had seen a few Titans at the club, their blue skin clashing with their green hair. I knew Titans loved Ioians, so it wouldn't surprise me if it had been one of them. Titans were well known for taking what they wanted, regardless of manners or decorum. It made me sick to think of all the people who had been touched by a Titan.

"How dare you touch the—" I lashed out before I realized Roald was the one who had touched me.

"Your Majesty, we must go. Your father needs you."

"But it's my birthday. Alard came all the way from Mars. Can't it wait until tomorrow?" I was in full princess pout mode. It usually worked on Roald.

"Absolutely not. We're leaving now."

"Ugh, you're no fun. I want to have fun and dance."

"I'll allow one more dance while I grab your belongings. Don't make me come find you again." Roald turned briskly before walking away.

"What a party pooper. We haven't even been here for an entire day." I muttered to Roald's back. Looking at my forearm, I noticed I had received four calls from the royal mansion. Having the doctors implant a screen onto my forearm was the best thing ever. Sure, I'd made them do it to commoners first to make sure it didn't, I don't know, kill them or anything. *Maybe it was important. No one ever calls me from the mansion. That's Roald's job.* Not feeling in the mood to dance anymore, I stomped off to the coat check.

I was still fuming about being taken away from the club on my birthday. I barely registered what Roald was saying as we sat in the back of the Limber, the Ioian version of Earth's Lamborghini. Daddy had it specially made with a back seat so I could be transported around the moon. The purple color sparkled under the lights. As it should, since there were ground up earth diamonds in the paint. A small price to pay to make sure your only child was happy.

Arriving at the mansion, I only saw one vehicle in the long, circular driveway. It was an ordinary transport vehicle with no markings on the sides. I considered not even waiting for Roald to open my door, with how mad I was at Daddy for calling me away from the club. He knew how I felt about dancing. Of course I didn't do it myself, as I wouldn't be caught dead opening my own door. As

I waited, I considered how bad it must be for him to call me home. It couldn't be too bad; we have genetics which allow our bodies to regrow damaged body parts, and we live a long time.

As he opened the door, I stepped out without taking Roald's hand. *I'm sure he knows how mad I am by not taking his hand.* With no response, he followed me in as we walked toward the front door.

Marci, my personal butler, opened the door to let us in. Her expression told me nothing about what was going on.

"Do you want to change before you see the king?"

"No. If he's bad enough to justify me coming home from the club early, then I can see him like this." I swore I saw Marci roll her eyes, but she wouldn't dare defy me.

"Where is he? In his office?" I walked to the wing of the house which held the office and other royal gathering places.

"No, he's in his room overlooking the garden."

Hmm, maybe he's not okay. He never sees people, even me, in his room.

"Thank you. And Marci, will you please make me a glass of Titan chocolate?"

As we walked to the king's personal room, I stood waiting for Roald to engage the door by being scanned. I had access, but I would never let it scan me. Yes, I had an implant for my intercell placed in my forearm, but the scanner kept a record to compare to the next time I was scanned. While that was how it detected the disease in my mother, I didn't want anyone, especially those council members, to be able to bring up a scan of me. Who knows what they would do with it. They were creepy and old.

Marci sighed. "Princess, did you not hear a word I said earlier? Are you sober?"

I turned to yell at her since she knew good and well I don't drink, but the look in her eyes belied sadness. "Yes, Marci. Of course I'm sober. Sorry, what were you saying?

"Your father was in an accident. We need to consider our next actions, which could mean you taking over the throne."

I'm going to be the queen! I get to tell everyone what to do! I can't wait.

"May I suggest you go change before meeting with your father?" Roald asked again as he looked over my club attire, a purple see-through body suit with a bikini made from fabric which mimicked a Chamaeleo, an Io-based reptile whose skin changes colors based on how they're feeling. The story goes some Earth chameleons snuck on a ship long ago and made their way to Io. Because some climates on Io were supposedly similar to Earth, they were able to survive and thrive. Over the years, they evolved to what we call the Chamaeleo.

"Give it up. He knows what I wear to the club, and this is who I am."

"As you are, then."

"Obviously."

I wasn't ready for what I saw. My father, the king, was in bed with one leg in a stasis tube, and I couldn't see the other. His head rested on a somewhat raised pillow. A young Martian woman stood near him taking vitals from a machine which looked about 100 years old. His head was bandaged, and there was a clump of hair on the floor.

"Daddy, are you okay?" I rushed to his side.

Normally, I'm either begging for something, pouting about not being able to do something, or ignoring him. Seeing him like this made me almost feel guilty by my normal attitude. *Almost.*

"Your father was in a serious accident, so he may not be able to speak much," the young woman told me.

"Roald, where's Daddy's normal doctor? What is this machine? Why is there hair on the floor? Who is this *woman?*"

"Nice to meet you too, Princess Tahva. My name is Botha, and I'm a doctor from Mars. Your father sent for me. And this machine is what I'm using to make sure he'll be fine. The hair, well I had to cut a piece of his scalp away because he had shards of glass under it."

"No offense," *All the offense,* "but why aren't we using his normal doctor and the normal medical supplies? Wouldn't he, I don't know, be able to regenerate faster?"

"While normally the case, there are some extenuating circumstances prohibiting us from using more modern, *local,* methods of healing him."

The way she said "local" like it was beneath her had my hackles raised. We are the most advanced moon of all the moons. Some Martian talking down to me, well technically up since she was much shorter, would not take place.

My father struggled to sit up.

"Mr. Xi, please lay back down." Botha placed her hand on his shoulder.

He shrugged it off before speaking. "Tahva, please stop. Botha was a good friend of your mother's, and I trust her with my life. I don't know how much Roald told you about the situation, but we have to tread lightly."

Looking at Roald, I realized I had missed a lot more during the transport ride than I originally thought.

"I know what he said, but we have the best medical here. Why don't I have Roald take you to the royal hospital?" I was getting frustrated with my father for not listening to me. It was always this way with him. Just because I was a princess didn't mean I was stupid.

All three yelled 'No' at the same time.

"Umm, okay, but why not?"

"Because the royal hospital is interconnected with everything. For the time being, we must keep this quiet. Now, do you want to know what my injuries are, or are you going to continue trying to fight us?"

It wasn't every day my father spoke to me like this, but when he did, I knew to listen and do what he said. I sat, already planning how to redecorate the office when I became queen.

CHAPTER 2

"Captain, report to the bridge. I repeat, Captain, report to the bridge." Markus' voice came over the on-ship transmitter.

I lifted my head from the bunk, but it had merely been an hour since I'd laid down. After working 45 hours straight at the controls dodging the solar police, all I asked for was 3 hours of down time. *What is it this time?* The last time I had been summoned like this it had turned my world upside down.

As the bridge door slid closed behind me, instead of approaching my chair, I turned to the source of the voice from the transmitter. "Markus, what's going on?"

"Good morning, Captain. Isn't it a nice day?"

"Less pleasantries, more information." I didn't mean to sound so gruff. I like Markus, but I'm getting too old for these long missions.

Handing me an energy coffee, Markus turned back to the controls. "We intercepted a message the Solar Police received about where we were going, so I need to confirm we are to go to escape plan A."

"You woke me to tell me after all those hours spent running from them, they still found us?"

"It appears so, Captain." Markus looked around the bridge before lowering his voice. "We may have someone on the ship who is aiding them."

"I was thinking the same thing. You know what? Instead of going to plan A, let's go with plan E."

Markus blinked twice. "Are you sure, Captain? But—"

I put my hand up to stop where he was going. "I know, I know."

"But Captain, it's only been six months."

"Markus, I know. I have to face it at some point."

"I don't think she blames you…necessarily."

"Yeah, way to be reassuring. Please put in the coordinates and let me get some more sleep."

"Captain?"

"Yes Markus?" I was tired and not really wanting to go back to Earth, but what was needed is more important than what was wanted.

"With all the heat lately, I think we should stay on Earth for a bit, at least until we can get some work that doesn't take us as close to the police as this last run."

"I'll consider it, now let me sleep."

"Roger that, we should enter Earth's orbit in 12 hours."

Great. Earth. There was a good reason I hadn't been back in so long, and I have to face her again eventually. I wish it got easier. Death does things to a person, though.

***

I woke up as we were passing Earth's moon. No matter how many times I saw it from the bridge, Earth still called to me, and its beauty still took my breath away.

"Good to be home, eh Captain?"

"It's been a long time, hasn't it? Are you going to see your mom?"

Markus' mom lived in New Sydney and made the best lamingtons in all of Australia. At least the crew thought she did. Her coconut and chocolate sauce covered butter cakes were to die for. It was something Jasmine never could perfect, so I always got my fill at Markus' mom's place.

"Have you called Jasmine to let her know you're coming?"

"Nope, but I should since I need a ride from the port."

"You know I could take you out there."

"I know, but if I show up, I may end up on the wrong end of one of her traps."

Markus chuckled as he focused on entering Earth's atmosphere. "20 minutes until we land in Auckland."

"Well, I have 20 minutes to call and make sure she won't kill me when we land."

"She probably won't kill you, maim maybe, but not kill. After all, you're family." He turned toward the screens to ensure a smooth and uneventful landing.

Dreading the call but also looking forward to seeing them again, I went back to my quarters.

"Jasper? Is it you?"

The first thing I saw was red hair followed by a blur of brown before her face came in focus.

"Yeah Jasmine, hey, I know it's late notice, but I'm landing in Auckland in about 20 minutes. If you're busy, I can have Markus drop me off at the homestead." It wasn't until she responded I realized I had been holding my breath.

"No way. You know what Markus' momma would do if she found out I took her son away from her for one more minute. The girls also want to see you." The sadness in her eyes was softer than when I left the last time, but it was still there.

"Jasmine, I need to get ready for landing. You know Markus can't do everything himself." *He can do everything himself.*

"See you in about 30 minutes." Jasmine disconnected her intercell.

I threw everything I needed into a duffle and sat on the bed. In no time, I heard the engine thrusters change their pitch and the slight bump of us landing. *Markus is good at his job.*

I had barely ducked out of the ships loading door before two excited little red-headed girls jumped on me. I dropped my duffle to pick up both girls at once. Putting the oldest on my shoulders, I picked up my duffle again.

"Welcome home, Uncle Jasper," the older sister, Jannie, told me as her younger sister, Juju, nestled in my arm. "Thank you, Jannie. Where's your mom?"

"She told us she was going to be slower than us, so we should go ahead."

Looking up, I easily found Jasmine. Even though she was shorter than I was, her 6'5" height, bright red hair, and darkly tanned skin made her stand out among the tourists and locals waiting to leave or meet arrivals. I approached Jasmine with a girl on each shoulder, like I was carrying two bags of squirmy potatoes. Even though I was almost 7 feet tall, I knew they wouldn't fall off. This was a game we had played since they were toddlers.

"Leaving your kids to fend for themselves now, I see." I dropped my duffle to hug Jasmine as we met.

"Eh, they have trackers. And who would want them, anyway? You know how much they eat and talk. Anyone trying to take them would give them right back."

We laughed as the girls looked confused. I'm glad to hear her laugh, but it seemed a little forced. I wish I could take her pain away.

"Why wouldn't someone want us?" Juju asked.

"No reason little one; your mom and I are joking." I reached for my bag, but Jasmine grabbed it first.

I knew something was up with her, I didn't know what, but there was something. Jasmine never carried my bag. She said it smelled too much like space. With her loss, I could understand why. I watched closely as we walked back to her transport.

CHAPTER 3

The next two months went by as normally as they could for me. I clubbed at night and slept during the day. Father was regaining strength in his remaining limbs, and his leg was growing back well. I must admit, Botha did seem to know what she was doing. I obviously won't tell her, but I can admit it to myself, in my room, with no one around.

I was getting ready to go out with some friends to a new club opening near the spaceport when Marci stopped me to let me know I was to report to the office immediately.

"Can't it wait? I'm on my way out." I flipped my pastel pink hair over my shoulder. I'd recently gotten it done, and there was no way I was going to miss the chance to show it off. I had to bring in a hairstylist all the way from Titan to do it the way I like it.

"I'm sorry, Ma'am, but it was a direct order from the king."

"Fine, whatever, but I'm not changing." As I walked down the stairs toward the office in a bright yellow bodysuit with cutouts and white, strappy flats, through the windows I noticed more vehicles than usual in the driveway. Talking to myself, "I wonder what's going on. Marci didn't say anything about other people being here."

Roald was standing right outside the office with his hands clasped behind his back. He didn't say anything, so I assumed he hadn't heard me talking to myself.

"Do you know what's going on?" I stopped in front of him.

Not responding, he faced the scanner to start the process in opening the way into the office.

The room went silent as I entered. Expecting only my father and the regency council, I was surprised to see so many different entities in the same room. There were Martians, fellow Ioians with silver skin, pastel hair, and ice-blue eyes, and Titans. There were even a few Humans scattered among the group with their boring skin and hair and so short, I mean what are they? Maximum 6 figs? Wait, they don't use figs, they use feet. *See, I did know something about Humans.*

My father sat behind his desk. Over the last two months, the brightness I was used to seeing in his eyes before his accident had returned. Today however, they were back to the dullness I saw right after his last accident. His hair was pulled away from his face, showing a bruise on his temple. One arm was in a sling, and he was missing some fingers.

Putting on my best doting daughter's face for the imagers, I ran to his side. "Oh, Father! What happened to you?"

I can hear him chuckle through our mind link, *"Nice show, Tahva, nice show. I like the outfit. When did you plan on leaving?"*

"Soon, but Marci said this was important, so I stayed."

"It is, Tahva, it is. There has been another incident, and it is imperative that I take motions to protect you. This conference is about your future and, honestly, the future of the entire moon." The room went silent in anticipation of what he was about to say.

I couldn't wrap my brain around his comment about there being another incident. He had been getting better, and I don't know if he had even left the house since his first accident. My father was not normally accident prone, in fact, outside of the last two months, I don't remember him ever being severely injured or having injuries lasting for more than a day or two.

***

The king stood shakily and cleared his throat before speaking. "Tahva, as my only child, and the rightful heir to the throne of Io, we—myself, and the regency council— have decided your time for ruling is approaching. With everything going on, I believe it's time for me to vacate my seat to you, so you may reign true for many years."

A collective gasp echoed throughout the room as everyone looked from the king to the soon to be queen. It was glorious, all eyes on me, images taken for the news circuit. I preened and strutted until I saw one of the regency council members smirking.

What is he smirking about? I'm about to become his boss.

My father placed his hands on the desk. "Tahva, as you know, there are many rules regarding becoming queen. Training with different individuals to hone skills from fighting to diplomacy."

"It will be no problem. I've been doing some already." I swore I heard, 'On the dance floor, maybe' from someone in the audience, but when I looked, I couldn't determine who had said it. No bother, I will soon be their boss too, and when I find out who it was, there will be consequences.

One of the royal council members stepped forward. He was one of the taller ones. His stringy, pastel green hair hung to his shoulders, and the blue robe he wore clashed terribly with his hair. It wasn't even like he *had* to wear the blue robe. Most of them didn't wear robes but normal clothing. Trying to remember his name, I knew it started with a N. Must not be too important, but in the future, I should probably at least know their names.

"Your Highness, we have complete faith you will learn the ways of the throne before you take over. However, there is one rule we feel must be discussed immediately. The rule is in order for a princess to become queen, she must take a consort. This is to protect

14

the realm as well as yourself. With you being married, you'll have someone to look over you, as well as someone to help stop any potential spies from getting close."

I heard the clicks of the imager, and I'm sure they caught me with my mouth agape. *The audacity of them to think I need to have a man in my life to be a good queen. Gag me with a spork.*

"Regency Council, before my father leaves his position, maybe we should consider changing some rules, as this one is outdated and no longer appropriate."

"No, Tahva, I will not change it. You need a companion." I could hear small giggles from the crowd and the clicking of imagers as I stood there with my fists tightly clinched.

"But Daddy, I'm more than capable of ruling alone, and I have Roald with me."

"Leave us please." At the king's request, everyone but Roald left the room, leaving the three of us.

"Tahva, it's time to slow down, take responsibility, and have someone significant in your life. Roald will be leaving with me when we have found someone to be with you. You don't have to marry him right away, but you need someone in your life to help protect and support you." He reached into the top drawer of his desk and pulled out a digital brochure. "I think this will be your best option. I've already made an appointment for you tomorrow at 13:15. It's located at the space docks, and Roald knows how to get there."

"Yes, Daddy." Looking at the brochure, I realize it's for Matching Galaxies LLC, a matchmaking company. *Over my dead body will I be matched with some loser.*

CHAPTER 4

"What type of job is it?" I asked Markus over the intercell. He received notification about a new contract a client wanted us to take on. As I waited for him to answer, I looked through the kitchen window at Jasmine walking between the stove and the table with fluffy pancakes. I could also hear the giggles and pitter-pattering of feet as the girls chased Jasmine's newest research project, raising and caring for quokkas. I thought of them as her furry new charges. Their little nails tip-tapped on the porch as they ran into the house followed by the girls. Coming around the corner were two small animals with brown fur that lightened closer to their skin. Their noses twitched like a rabbits' at the smell of the pancakes. Their little triangle ears moved like tiny satellite dishes as they heard my voice.

It had been about two months since we landed on Earth, and I was going stir crazy. In fact, I think everyone was. I know Tak made sure each weapon had been cleaned at least twice, if not more. I'm sure the police had better things to do, so I was glad Markus finally found a job, or at least a possible job.

"It looks like a simple pick up and drop, but it's a long-range job. I'm trying to get a couple other jobs lined up so we can make a couple stops along the way and make some extra money."

"How far?"

Jasmine waved me in, letting me know brekky was ready.

I held up one finger to let her know it would be a minute.

"It looks like a long client transport from Mars to Triton for sure. Then, I have a trip possibly lined up of materials from Triton back toward Europa. It seems they're finally trying to terraform Europa."

"I like material jobs, usually pays well because they're under a time crunch."

"I was thinking the same thing. Well, I'll get back to arranging some other jobs."

"Thanks, Markus. Let me know what comes up. Tell your mom hi for me."

"You know I already did. Right now, our timeline is about four days. If it speeds up, I'll let you know."

"Yeah, four days should be enough time to get the space cops off our tail. At least, if everything we're doing is on the up and up."

"This time it is." Markus said his goodbyes as he laughed. Not everything we do is completely legal, but it's good to have some legitimate jobs to keep the cops from circling.

I walked back into the kitchen to see all three sitting at the table eating pancakes.

"Did you leave any for me?"

Juju giggled as I sat next to her. I took three pancakes and began eating.

As I was finishing up the last pancake, Jasmine told the girls to go play. Looking up at her, I waited for what I thought she was going to say.

"Jasper, how long are you going to be here?"

"I was talking to Markus, and it looks like we will be here for another 4 days, at least. He's lining up jobs."

"Markus lines up jobs while you're, what? Sunbathing and playing with the girls?" Jasmine cleaned up the dishes.

"Exactly what a captain does, sunbathes and makes sure their crew is good at their job," I said. Before I realized what had come out of my mouth. Jasmine's husband Raf had been captain of his ship, and while his crew was good at what they did, it didn't help him. Jasmine must have caught on as well because it looked like she was about to tear up.

Standing, I walked over to her as she still held the dishes. I took them from her and put them into the sink. Wrapping my arms around her, I held her while she cried. "I wish there was something I could do Jasmine; you know I would if I could."

Through her sniffles I heard her respond, "I know, I wish there was something. I miss him so much."

Since I didn't know how she felt, never having lost someone like she had, I held her. "I know you do; I know."

After a few minutes, she stopped crying and stepped away from me, drying the tears with her sleeves. "I'm scared, Jasper."

"Of what? You have a great job, the girls go to a good school, and we own the land."

"Of losing you. Don't pretend you wanted to come home. No, something happened up there, and you had to come back to Earth."

"Nothing happened, and because nothing happened, we decided to come back. I'm not going to sugar coat it; we had the cops on our tail, and Markus and I decided it was best to have some down time."

"When are you going to stop all this? We have so much money, and you have a spaceship you could legally run without worry. You could settle down, start a family."

"Jasmine, as much as I love coming back to Earth and seeing you three, you know my life is in the stars."

Jasmine got a faraway look in her eyes, as if remembering something, or maybe another conversation she'd had.

"Raf said the same thing. He was the most at home in the stars and look what happened to him."

I wish I could tell her I'm not Raf, and I would be fine. But I couldn't lie to her because she knew my trips were more dangerous than anything Raf had done.

"Look, I do want to settle down at some point, but I want to be with someone who either doesn't care if I'm gone all the time or is willing to travel with me. I can't give up everything I've worked for."

"I'm tired, Jasper. The job is winding down, and we have successfully completed the last part of it. I don't know what I'm going to do. There aren't many jobs for a zoologist in all the Oceania region, let alone Australia."

"Come with me then? Leave the girls with Raf's parents and come with me, explore the stars for a little while." I thought about what I was going to say next. "You know Raf wanted you to travel with him, so come with me."

"I don't know. Part of me wants to see where he died, to visit the stars you both loved so much. I don't know if I can face Raf's parents though. I haven't spoken to them since the funeral."

"Of course you can. You have their grandbabies, and you know Raf wouldn't want you to have a strained relationship with them." I reached for her hand. "We'll figure it out together. When does the job end? Do you have a timetable for it yet?"

"You say that, but they still blame me for his death."

"Jasmine do you really believe that? He was in space, you were here, how could they blame you?"

"Because they blame you, and by extension, me for him being in space. To answer your other question, in about three months the latest reports will show if the numbers are high enough for the project to be considered complete."

As I was about to say something else, my phone rang. Patting her shoulder, I answered it while walking out the kitchen door. "Markus, what do you have for us?"

"They sent the contract over, so I'll review it and let you know. Enjoy the time with your family." He hung up, and I decided to do exactly what he said.

***

Over the next two days, I was in communication with Markus, but the jobs weren't lining up like we had hoped. It was expensive to fly to the outer moons, so we liked to have as many jobs lined up as we could for each trip. I started to think about what Jasmine, and I had talked about, about settling down and having a family. I had my nieces and didn't want my own children, especially with my job, but having someone by my side wouldn't be too bad.

"Jasper, your intercell is going off," Jasmine called from the door while I was playing outside with the girls.

"Thanks." I told the girls I would be right back.

"Markus, tell me good news."

"I have good news, and I need a favor. The good news is we have enough jobs lined up now to make it worth our time."

"What's the favor?"

"You know how my mom has been trying to get me to settle down and stay Earthside, right?"

Markus' mom was getting older, and with Markus being the only child, it didn't surprise me she was pushing him to stay local.

"Yeah, and?"

"She set up this interview at a matchmaking place, but in trying to get out of it, I told her I wouldn't go unless you did."

I knew where this was going, and I was about to tell him to shove it.

"Okay, and?"

"We are set to leave in 48 hours for these jobs, so my mom made each of us an appointment. And before you say no, will you please go with me? She put down a deposit and everything. I didn't think she was this serious."

"Markus, we've known each other since we were kids. If it makes your mom happy, I'll go with you, but don't expect me to ever let you live this down."

"Captain, you know I don't expect you to."

The topic broached, Markus gave me directions to the business, and I hung up considering what I had gotten myself into.

Walking back into the house, I let Jasmine know what was going on.

"Hey, don't get too excited, but I'm going to a matchmaking business tomorrow."

"Um what? Can you repeat?"

"Markus' mom, Cynthia, signed him up. He thought he could get out of it by telling her he wouldn't go without me, and you know how scary she is. I don't want to be on her bad side, so I agreed."

"Can the girls and I go with you? We could go shopping while you're in your meeting with them."

"Sure, why not? The appointment is tomorrow. Let me call Markus and let him know you three will be coming with us."

Jasmine clapped her hands and hugged me before she ran outside to play with the girls. I had a feeling she and Cynthia may have been in communication to set this up.

CHAPTER 5

"Princess, it is time for your appointment," Roald announced as he walked into my room.

A small part of me was surprisingly excited about this appointment. Less about meeting someone and more about proving them wrong about needing someone. If I never matched with anyone, I wouldn't be able to find a consort, and I should have more power to change the rules. Why did a bunch of old men think I needed someone to 'protect' me when I can protect myself? Maybe it's wishful thinking, but I know my father, and I know I can bend the rules enough to rule alone.

I know my father, the king wants what's best for me, but the love he shared with my mom was unique, something few experienced, especially since they had been betrothed to each other. Mother and Father were destined to marry before they were even born. When Father's parents married, they began looking for a suitable family for their son or daughter to marry into. Even though it was a betrothal, Mother always told me she could have walked away if Father was a bad man or mistreated her. Looking over at the picture of her, I wish I could talk to her about it. She understood my desire to be independent and unique.

"Hey, I'm ready." I stood from my small writing desk wearing a smart black pantsuit with a pink camisole under the jacket. My hair was in a plait Marci finished about 30 clicks before Roald announced himself.

"You look good, Princess."

"Thank you. I figured if I was ever going to put my best foot forward, this should be the time, right?"

And if I show up looking like the rightful heir and future queen, maybe they will take me seriously when I say I don't need to be with someone and can rule by myself.

"I want to reiterate what your father said previously; this is non-negotiable. You must have a consort if you want to become queen."

"Since when did you become a rule follower?" I smirked at Roald before turning away from him. We rode the rest of the way in silence to the space docks, pulling up in front of a small white building with light green trim with a big sign reading, "Matching Galaxies LLC".

"Roald, stay here. I can do it myself."

"But Princess…"

I stopped him before he could start. "This is a one-story building. I'm not going to run out the back in these heels. I'll do as my father asked me."

Roald looked at me suspiciously before nodding his head in acknowledgment.

When I walked up to what I hoped was the front door, I waited for it to open before realizing it was the type you had to physically touch. *Gag, why must I do this? Maybe I should have had Roald come with me after all.* Looking back for a second, I straightened my shoulders and pushed the door open.

"Welcome to Matching Galaxies LLC, where we provide a match made in space. My name is Meta, do you have an appointment, or are you walking in?" A chipper young Titan with black hair sat behind the receptionist desk. *At least she knew how to dye her hair.*

"Yes, I have an appointment."

"Great, what's your name?"

How does she not know who I am? I'm the princess.

"I am Tahva Xi."

"Let me look to see if you have an appointment."

Of course I have an appointment. I literally just told you I do.

"Here you are, great. Take a seat, and the matchmaker will be with you in a minute."

She doesn't know who I am, and I have to wait? Who do they think they are?

Turning before sitting, I spoke up, "Oh, Meta, right? Can I have a sparkling water?"

"Yes, I'll have one brought out to you."

"Thank you." *And this is how you exert dominance. I don't even want water.*

Less than 5 clicks later, the glass door opened, and an Ioian came out holding a water and called my name. I was impressed. Her dark blue suit contrasted nicely against her silver skin. Even her heels matched her outfit. This was a woman who knew how to dress. Maybe it wouldn't be as easy as I thought it would be to pressure her into letting me go without finding a match. Standing, I pulled my jacket down and walked over to her.

"Princess Tahva, I'm pleased to meet you. I'm Fareh, and I'll be working with you." She handed me the water.

"Thank you, but maybe you should teach your staff to recognize royalty." I scoffed as I sat in the plush chair and crossed my legs.

Fareh eyed me before answering, "I'm sorry. Meta is new to Io. We moved her from the Titan location. We try to—"

"I don't care about your business practices. Can we do this so I can leave and go on about my life?"

"Yes, of course. I understand you must be busy, with all the clubbing and dancing you do. I have a few short questions, and you can be on your way."

"Wow. First off, rude. I do a lot more than clubbing and dancing. I am well educated, contrary to what you may believe. I can also do some work if needed. Can we get this started with this so I can be done?" I leaned back in the chair, believing I was in control of this appointment. I was a little irked by her comment about clubbing, but I know my business is all over the circuit.

"First question. Do you want to move off moon?"

"Absolutely not. As you know, I'm the princess, soon to be Queen of Io, so due to my royal duties, I would be unable to move off moon."

"I didn't realize there would be a transfer of power soon. My condolences."

Crap, I guess everyone will know now. "It's alright, he's not dying; he's simply giving me the power."

"Interesting. Question two. How do you feel about children?"

"Eww." *Probably too aggressive as a response.* I cleared my throat. "What I mean is, maybe for other people, but can you imagine me having children? No, thank you."

"If I may I ask? If you don't want children, who will rule after you?"

"Right now, not my problem." *Who is she to ask me such a personal question, one I hadn't even thought about yet?*

"How would you feel if your intended match already has children?"

"I don't know, I wouldn't be completely against the idea. But I'm not willing to be someone's second choice, especially with them bringing baggage. I would expect the children to come with a nanny or some other caregiver."

"Thank you for clarifying. Last question. Do you have a preference on planet or moon of origin for your match?"

"Since I've dated probably every acceptable Ioian, I doubt you'll be able to find someone for me from this moon." I lowered my voice. "As long as they aren't Titan, I don't care. Can you imagine how much we would clash going out?"

I couldn't tell if the look Fareh gave me was of disdain or amusement, but I didn't care.

"Perfect, those are all the questions we have for you. Your bodyguard has already provided the rest of the necessary information."

He has, has he? We shall be having a conversation about how bold he has become recently. I stood to walk out the door when Fareh stopped me.

"I have one final question before you leave, okay?"

Whatever gets me out of here faster. "Yes, of course."

"Good, how do you feel about a match who isn't royalty?"

Something about the way she asked made me feel like she had something up her tailored sleeves, but I couldn't pinpoint what.

"Depending on the situation, it may be acceptable. There aren't any rules against it, as far as I know" *She thinks I'll match with someone. I'm a princess; there aren't many people who could keep up with me.*

***

"What do I even wear to this type of thing?" I asked over my shoulder as I dug through my closet full of clothes.

"Anything clean; it doesn't matter."

"Fine, I'll wear a button up and a pair of flight pants. I am a pilot and all."

I got dressed and walked out to the dining room to see Jannie and Juju coloring at the table. Ruffling their hair, I turned to face Jasmine. "Well, how do I look?"

"Looking great, Uncle," Jannie answered without looking up.

"Thank you, but I was mostly asking your mom."

Reaching up. Jasmine fixed the top button before speaking. "You look great. I'm sure Mom and Dad would be proud of you."

Seeing her eyes mist up, I hugged her. "You know they're proud of both of us."

"I know. It's time to go." She turned toward the kitchen to usher the girls into the car.

I walked out to the Ranger to make my way to Markus' and then downtown.

One great thing about the Ranger was it transported itself, so I could focus on the mission briefings with Markus while the girls sat in the back. The first mission looked like an easy pick up and drop off of some diplomat or something. The money was good. I could afford to not only give bonuses to the crew but maybe buy more land for Jasmine. Land was the one thing no matter what happened, it would be there. The value of land was something Mom and Dad instilled in us from an early age, and I was able to buy a nice piece of land before I bought the spaceship. I never understood how she could be so grounded while I needed to be among the stars. I wonder how much of it was because of Raf's death.

A voice announcing I had arrived at the office stopped me from thinking more about the day everything changed. I looked out the window to see a blue building with white trim with large white letters declaring the business's name. "Matching Galaxies LLC" *What an interesting name since it's on Earth.*

"This is where Markus and I leave you three. Be careful, and we'll see you in about an hour?"

"Sounds good. Girls, are you ready to go shopping?" There were happy screams as Jannie and Juju jumped out of the car and each held one of their mom's hands.

Walking through the door we were immediately greeted by a young man. "Pleasure meeting you, Mr. Moriarty and Mr. Jackson, here are a couple waters. The director is finishing up a conference with a coworker, and then she'll be able to meet with you, Mr. Moriarty. Mr. Jackson, the director said you will be meeting with me, okay?"

"That's perfectly fine, thank you. Please call me Markus." Markus shook the young man's hand.

"Thank you, but please call me Jasper. Mr. Moriarty was my father. Um… what was your name again?"

"Sorry, I didn't introduce myself. I'm Khai. If you need anything, please let me know." Khai turned to another room and led Markus away.

I sat in silence drinking my water while I looked around the office. The room was painted light blue and had plush brown couches. The music was soft and did not distract but was rather soothing.

"Mr. Moriarty, are you ready?" An older woman walked out from behind a room divider designed with classic New Zealand imagery.

"Yes, like I told Khai, please call me Jasper." As I approached her, she shook my hand, and I was surprised by her strength.

She smiled. "And you can call me Sith. And before you ask, yes, my parents enjoyed classic movies."

Smiling back, I was instantly at ease with Sith. I took a seat in front of her desk. "My parents did as well, especially the movies created in New Zealand. At least I wasn't named after a hobbit or something."

Sitting at her desk, Sith pushed a button, opening her comm device. "I'm sure you're busy, and I understand Mrs. Jackson may have sprung this on you last minute, so I'm glad you decided to meet with us anyway. I have three simple questions, and you can be on your way."

"I have nothing to do as I have a good ship crew, but I usually spend the extra time with my nieces, so I appreciate this being quick."

"Mr... I mean Jasper, do you have a preference on entity you wish to be matched to?"

"Not at all. My crew is made up of a diverse group of individuals, and I believe they all have their own strengths."

"Excellent. Do you want to stay on earth or are you open to travelling?"

"Considering my profession, I prefer to travel, or at least not stay in one place all the time. It would be hard for me to be with someone who was a complete homebody."

"Thank you, and the last question, how do you feel about children? Do you want your own? How do you feel about a prospective partner having them?"

"I don't particularly want children, but I'm okay if it happens naturally or if my partner already has children. However, I do have a somewhat special condition."

"What's your condition?"

"If I was to have a match who does not live in New Zealand, or even on Earth, they must be willing to, at least, meet my sister and her two daughters. I'm their only family, so we're a package deal, even if they don't end up living with me."

Sith paused a minute before responding, as if she was formulating a plan. "Jasper, finding a match who accepts your family won't be a problem. I respect your loyalty."

CHAPTER 6

Roald woke me up early the day following my matchmaking appointment with a letter.

Who does written correspondence anymore? It is 2430. As I took it in my hands, I noticed a wax seal on the flap, securing it closed. Before I could ask, Roald handed me an antique letter opener.

"Here, use this on the wax."

Thanks, like I don't know what to do. Opening the letter, I saw it was from Matching Galaxies LLC. Under the business name was their logo, "Matches made in space". Skimming the words, I dropped the letter. I wasn't sure how to feel. Part of me was excited, but mostly, I was pissed. I thought I'd figured out how to get away from this. I was not easy to be with.

"Princess Tahva Xi, it is our pleasure at Matching Galaxies to impart we have found a bachelor we believe will be perfect for you. Please sign this preliminary contract stating you understand the initial rules. Once we have received your signature, we will send you additional information.

P.S. You can let Roald know you will be staying on moon for this meeting as they will be traveling to you."

"Well Princess, what does it say?"

"It says they found me someone, and 'they' will be travelling here within two weeks. I don't have enough time to get ready, and what if he's hideous? And who are 'they'? I don't want kids, and I told them." *My plan was not working the way I thought it would.*

"Everything will work out as it should. You'll be fine. I have faith. Do you want me to read the contract before you sign it?"

"No, thank you, I can do it myself."

Roald started listing off the things I had on my calendar for the day. I couldn't focus because not only was I trying to figure out what the contract said, but in less than 14 days, my life may no longer be my own, and I was furious.

I skimmed the rules. There were eight of them, and I'd never been good with rules. I'm a princess after all. They seemed to be all about the deadline to be married and what happened if we decided not to stay together. Nothing I thought I necessarily needed to worry about yet.

***

As I finished up the inventory list Markus handed me before he went out on the town, a courier called my name. When I stepped from my makeshift office, a man with a backpack handed me a letter. Opening it, I immediately saw "Matching Galaxies LLC – Matches made in space" and assumed it would be a rejection letter.

"Mr. Jasper Moriarty, it is our pleasure at Matching Galaxies to impart we have found a bachelorette we believe will be perfect for you. Please sign this preliminary contract stating you understand the initial rules. Once we have received your signature, we will send additional information.

P.S. As you own your own spaceship and will be travelling on business near where this individual lives, please check the box which

*states Matching Galaxies LLC will assist in fuel costs but is not
responsible for any damage which may result from the trip."*

*At least I'll have some of my mission's fuel paid, meaning more money
in our pockets. I'm sure the crew will enjoy a stopover wherever we have to go to
meet my new 'bride'.*

The contract was boiler plate with no more specifics about
who I was to marry. There were eight rules covering what we needed
to do. The first rule was how long after meeting we needed to marry,
which was six weeks. If we decided to not get married by the
assigned date, we had to explain to the company why we postponed
it. There were three rules regarding what we could or could not do
before we were married. I thought it was weird, but this was the first
time I was given a contract for marriage, so I didn't know what to
expect. If we decided to not get married, we had to explain why,
individually and together. If we were to get married and later decide
to not stay together, we had to agree not to divorce for six months
following letting the company know about our intentions. The last
rule was interesting, and I read it twice to make sure I understood it.

*'Under no circumstances shall any information learned about the
company, or the intended spouse be divulged to law enforcement, family, friends, or
lawyers.'*

"What are you reading?" Markus asked as he got back.

"It appears I've been matched with someone, and they aren't
on this planet."

"Great. Are you going to meet with her?"

"Actually, I think we're all going. Apparently, since she isn't
on Earth, the company wants me to use my spaceship to meet her,
and since I don't fly alone, I figured we could arrange for it to
happen during one of the trips. I'm supposed to get more details
later."

"Sounds good. I enjoy myself some R and R."

"Markus, did you get anything from Matching Galaxies?"

"Yeah, it was nothing though. Apparently, I didn't match with anyone, so they have me on a waitlist."

I've known Markus long enough to know when he's lying, and he was definitely lying.

***

Whatever excitement I'd had died when I got the second letter two days before I was to meet 'my match'. The letter gave basic details, apparently his name was Jasper, a name I had not heard before. I figured I would sign the document, get the specifics, and tell them I couldn't do it. My father found out about it before I did, so I couldn't back out as easily.

"He's a Human with a family! I told them no kids." I stomped around the king's office.

"Yes, but they aren't his kids. They're his sister's. And they aren't even coming initially. He simply wants you to meet them at some point. So what if he's a Human? It isn't like you've met any suitable Ioians." Two of the four fingers which had been lost were growing back, but his arm was still in a sling. The only people in the room were the king, Roald, and me.

"But Daddy!" I put on my best pouty face.

The king nodded to Roald before speaking. "Listen Tahva, there's more to the story about my accident than you know. It wasn't an accident. Someone tried to kill me. It's Roald and I's hope when you take over the throne, whomever is trying to kill me leaves the royal family alone."

"Don't be dramatic. I read the report, and it says nothing about being an assassination attempt." *Maybe I hadn't read it; I had it read to me by Marci.*

"Do you think we put everything in the news circuit? If we want to find out who's responsible, we must keep some things to ourselves. Do you want to know what actually happened?"

I wasn't known for keeping things to myself, at least according to the news circuit.

"Of course I do."

My dad placed his hands on his desk and began his story.

"The night of your birthday party I went to meet a council member for dinner to discuss an upcoming construction project. We were planning on collaborating with Titan officials to terraform Europa, the smallest of Jupiter's four moons. I was meeting with him to discuss what percentage Io was going to put forward initially and what Io was going to get in return."

I knew terraforming was important because Io is becoming more and more urban. Normally it would be fine, but we need the minerals and other natural resources from Europa, as well research in case Europa, in the future, could eventually be a good location for Ioians to move. I had heard about it enough from meetings I had been forced to sit through.

"You had a meeting? What does this have to do with you getting hurt?"

"Tahva, do you want to know the story, or are you going to constantly interrupt me?"

"I'm sorry, please continue."

Roald looked shocked by my apology, but I know how my father can be when I interrupt him when he's talking about something important.

"The meeting went well. The council member was unsure if Io should be included in the terraforming at all because he didn't see any benefit coming from it. I explained not only will it help us in the future, but it could show everyone Io is not as isolated or as unsophisticated as many believe. We want to be part of the solar system, both economically and politically. It will make Io stronger, and it strengthens the royal council and the royal family. The council member felt it wasn't beneficial because there was no guarantee Europa could be terraformed, and if we spent too much of our resources on Europa when there are other moons we could easily work on, Io could fall to a stronger moon or planet.

"I reminded him there has not been an active conflict in the solar system in more than four centuries and the last was because Earth tried to take over Mars. Io was peaceful, and we always stayed out of conflicts not directly related to Io or our independence.

"I'm not proud of how I reacted when the council member raised his voice. I still don't understand why he was so upset. The deal had already been signed to do preliminary research and build a small space station for our scientists. This council member was livid, and he kept mumbling under his breath and saying things like, 'This has to happen' and 'What am I going to tell him'. I had no idea what was going on. I do know me telling him the deal was going as planned, and there was nothing he could do about it caused him to go into a rage.

"I decided it was time to leave because we were attracting attention, and you know how fast things can get into the circuit. I told my driver to take me back to the mansion. As I was about to leave, the council member grabbed me by the back of my robe. Before I could turn to tell him to unhand me, he whispered in my ear, 'You will pay for this' and let me go. I figured he was upset I didn't give in, so I didn't think much of it."

"All you did was upset one of the council members? It happens frequently, why is it an issue now?"

"I thought the same thing. I have been the king for a long time, and during my reign, I have caused my fair share of disagreements. However, what happened next caused me to rethink my assumption."

"What happened?" I didn't realize it, but I'd sat in the wing-backed chair he kept in his office and was on the edge of my seat listening to him, enraptured by his story. It was like one of those old earth movies I watched with Mom before she died.

"This is where it gets weird.

***

"We got into the transport. You had the Limber at the club. On the way back, I asked the driver to swing by the port because I had thought about something I wanted to check out before heading back to the mansion. When I arrived at the port, I had the driver go to our royal hangar. I asked the driver to wait while I checked it out. I got out of the transport and went over to the hangar door. When I opened the door, I heard voices, but I knew no one should be there. I walked in and yelled 'who's there', and two Titans came out from behind the ship. They didn't recognize me immediately, so I took advantage of it and asked them why they were there. They didn't answer but looked at each other before they asked me why I was there. I told them I was the king's personal assistant, and I was checking on the ship for the king because he was thinking about taking his daughter out for her birthday. They laughed and told me to mind my own business. When one turned around, I again asked why they were there. He was looking at me strangely, so I said, 'I'll go ask the quartermaster' and turned to leave. By the time I got to the transport, I could hear the men yelling something and told the driver to hurry back to the mansion.

"I called the owner of the port and told him what was going on. While I was explaining what the men looked like, the transport was hit by something. I never saw it coming. The transport was still moving, but when it was hit a second time, we were thrown over the Estes Cliffs. Thankfully, the transport had gelatin to cushion the impact, saving our lives, but it didn't keep the transport from taking damage. When we finally stopped, I checked on the driver and called Roald immediately."

"Roald was on the phone at the club; he didn't tell me why." The pieces clicked into place.

"Yes, he didn't want to alarm you. I had him bring you home but not tell you the extent of my injuries."

"I probably wouldn't have listened to him anyway, since I was mad about having to leave. It was my birthday."

"I know, Tahva, and it was never my intention to ruin your birthday." He held out the hand with all his fingers, and I grabbed it.

"What happened next?"

"When I talked to Roald and told him where I was, I reached out to Botha to let her know I was hurt. I didn't realize at the time how badly the driver and I were hurt, but I knew even if it was an accident, I wanted Botha there to ensure my health was taken care of. She's also a former soldier, so I knew she would protect me if needed."

"Wait, Botha was a soldier?"

"Yes, but that's not my story to tell."

"If you say so. But why are you leaving?"

"Because even though I'm healing, and I was able to get away before I was seriously injured, I may not be able to the next time. The first time something strange happened, I may have been able to pass it off, and maybe I wasn't targeted, but the second time I knew it had to be someone coming directly after me. I still don't know why, but I know I must leave."

"You didn't answer my question about why I have to get married?"

"Because we are keeping up appearances, and Roald and I think you being married will help in the event—" before he could finish his sentence, the main alarm sounded.

"Tahva, please go to the meeting and marry the man. If nothing else, please keep him around for the foreseeable future. According to the rules, you must marry within three months. Io has an allotted time it can go without a ruler. If you do not ascend the throne, someone from the regency ouncil will. Do not tell the council what's happening, do you understand?"

Roald pushed the king through the secret door he had in his office, the conversation ending abruptly.

"But wait, why are you leaving? What's going on?"

Roald answered as my father was already through the door, "Trust only Marci. She'll know how to get ahold of us if you need to. We don't know who's behind this, and at the moment, we think this is about your father, not you, but be watchful." Roald hugged me before disappearing behind the closing door.

I composed myself and stood in the office with a book in my hand when the door burst open with two members of the Regency Council. "Where is the king? We must speak with him immediately."

Looking as innocent as I could muster, I slowly blinked at them before answering. "He hasn't been here all day. I'm merely taking in some light reading."

The men looked at the book in my hand before looking over the office. Satisfied my father wasn't there, they left. I looked down and realized the book in my hand was "The History of Matchmaking in Ioian Culture." *Great, exactly what I need. I guess I'm meeting my husband in two days.*

***

After receiving the second letter detailing more information, I couldn't believe how quickly things had aligned. Pick up a traveler on Mars, fly out to Triton, take the materials to Europa, hop over to Io, meet this 'Tahva', explain how it wasn't going to work while my crew had some liberty time, and finish up the last two jobs before flying back to Earth, all on Matching Galaxies and my clients' dimes. Win-win if I don't say so myself.

Takeoff went smoothly, and the trip to Mars was uneventful. Once I arrived at the main port in the capital city, I waited on the *Stellar Kiwi*, my nimble but roomy spaceship. I guess roomy was overstating how big it was, but for the three of us it was plenty of room. The name came from a play on the words for stars and '*Kiwi*', which was what people from my country were called in the past, at least according to the history books I had to read during school.

"Crew, unload the supplies we have for Brutus, and I think he has some stuff for the other places we're hitting. While you work, I'll find our passenger."

"Sounds good, Captain."

The crew started unwrapping pallets of goods and moving them into position at the rear of the ship.

I walked into the complex. The minute I stepped through the airlock I found the Martian I was transporting. Not only was he the only one pacing and constantly looking around, but he only had one small bag. Most tourists bought everything they could carry and usually more. Also, Mars was laid back for the most part so for someone to pace, they were either nervous about travelling or waiting for someone.

"Mr. Tovak, hello. I am Captain—" I reached out to shake his hand. He looked at my hand before shaking his head.

"I know who you are. I have an important meeting on Triton, and I must insist we leave right now." He looked up at me, and the one thing I noticed right away was his eyes. Martians all had red skin and black hair and eyes, but his eyes were green, like the green hills of New Zealand.

"We'll leave when the supply exchange is completed and we get all the goods for the other runs. If you would follow me."

Even though he huffed when I said it may be longer than he'd thought, he followed me to the ship.

"I was unsure if this is your first trip to Triton, so I saved you this seat. It will have a wonderful view of the rings." I showed him the seat.

"No, it isn't, but I hope it's my last." The passenger sat and promptly fell asleep.

I wish my mind would turn off so I could fall asleep so quickly.

CHAPTER 7

Even after my father's explanation of what was going on, I still wasn't convinced someone was out to get him. Over something like building materials? It doesn't make sense. I've seen people get into fights over random stuff, but to try to kill the sitting king over a ship full of building materials? This whole thing seems ridiculous. Maybe there's more to it, and maybe Father was mistaken about someone trying to kill him.

But ever since his disappearing act, living alone in the mansion with just Marci, I thought maybe I should look into his claims. At least as much as I could since I didn't know much about what he did as king. Considering I'm about to be queen, I should probably learn more about it.

"Marci, can you please come here?" I yelled from the office door. Yes, I could have used the internal communication system, but even if I didn't exactly believe my father's assertions about being targeted for an assassination attempt, I was still going to be careful about being on anything trackable.

"Yes, Ma'am. What can I do for you? Do you need a drink or to get dressed?"

"I need two things. I need you to track down Botha. She's the doctor who was here for my mother." I trusted Marci, but I didn't know if she knew Botha was there for Father when he had his first injuries.

"I believe she's still on moon in case your father needed anything. And your second thing?"

So, she knew Botha had seen father when he had been injured.

"I need either you or someone you trust to teach me what to do to become queen and a wife. What books to read, what circuits I should be reading, what I should be doing. I'm flying blind, and I need your help."

It was the first time I think I ever actually asked someone for help other than to get ready to go out or something else selfish. I guess this was also a little selfish, but it was also for the betterment of the moon and our people.

"Princess, I can help you with becoming a queen, but I can't help you with your impending marriage."

"At least you can help me with one of the two things. Thank you, Marci."

For the last two days, all I did was go from my room to the kitchen and back. I refused to talk to anyone but the instructors and Marci. I realized I was nervous about meeting this Human 'Jasper'. What kind of name is Jasper anyway? It sounded like a pet's name. I felt vulnerable in a way I had never felt before without Roald's constant presence. As long as I could remember, he was always beside or behind me. After they left, I realized while I was still the party girl I'd always been, I needed to be more; if nothing else than to keep my family alive. I didn't like the position I was put in any more than I figured my father liked the position he was in.

***

The landing into Triton went smoothly, as it always does. Triton was a lawless place, so no one looked twice at my spaceship. I looked through the imagers to make sure no one was waiting right outside the ship to try to mug us. It only happened once, but I would rather it not happen again.

"Tovak, we have arrived." I had to shake him gently as he had slept the entire trip.

"Already? Great get me off this ship."

"You'll have to wait until the controller gives us clearance to open the door. I'll let you know when it's time to leave."

"Whatever, I hope it's quick as I have meetings to get to."

Less than five minutes later, Markus received the all-clear, and after checking again to make sure no one was going to ambush Tovak or my crew, I went back to our passenger to let him know it was time to leave.

"Good." And then he was gone, practically running out the door. I had never wanted to bad mouth a client before, but this guy was a real piece of work.

I caught a glimpse of what I thought was a weapon when he stood, but I'm not one to question what my clients do or have on them as long as they don't threaten myself or my crew. I watched out the window as he skirted what Triton considered customs and left in a black transport vehicle. *Good riddance.*

"Get the materials for Europa and let's head out. I don't want to be here any longer than we need to."

"Will do, Tak you're with me."

Markus and Tak, a Titan who has been part of the crew for almost as long as I have needed a crew, headed out to the transport vehicle pulling up to the ship.

While they worked, I kept my eye out for anyone who might want to steal what we were receiving on my ship. While I watched and waited, I thought about the last time we were on Triton.

It was a deal set up by a former gun runner. By former, I assume he isn't alive anymore after our last interaction. He contacted us to deliver a pallet of goods to Triton in exchange for materials needed by another client of ours. Everything looked good when we arrived on the planet, but after landing, we were surrounded by Tritonians who wanted to take the pallet off our hands. They weren't the ones we were delivering to, and they weren't asking nicely.

The landing zone had been clear, and there were no other ships, so Markus sat the ship down. While we were warned we could get a lot of attention because of what we were transporting, our record was good up to that point. We were confident we could drop off and pick up before anyone noticed we were there. It would be the last time I was so naïve.

Landing, we contacted the transport who would deliver the materials for our return trip and to pick up the materials we were delivering. They told us it would be 20 minutes, so we sat and waited. In the meantime, we hadn't noticed the transport coming in from the rear of the port. When we saw the transport for us coming out, the second transport suddenly tried to cut them off, with men jumping out of the transport with guns.

"What do you want to do?"

"Let's see what they do, but be ready, Markus. I don't want to give up this transport if we don't have to."

"Copy."

We continued to watch while a gun fight broke out between the transport we were supposed to meet up with and the hijackers. After a bit, it looked like things were winding down, and the second transport sped away after picking up the men who came with them. I told Markus to take Tak to check it out.

I watched them go, Tak with a weapon followed by Markus. The driver of the transport we were supposed to meet up with approached Markus, and they spoke for a minute before Markus and Tak returned to the ship.

"We're good to unload, but we have to do it quickly."

When Markus says something needs to be done quickly, I put the entire crew on it to make sure it happens. As the loads were being exchanged, I noticed another transport coming in, much faster than the first.

"We got to go. Two time it, now."

Markus looked over and noticed the transport arriving.

The transport arrived as we were finalizing locking the load into the storage bay on the ship. The first transport, now carrying the goods we delivered, was driving away, forgotten by the new one as they saw a ship they believed they could easily take over.

"We don't have time to close the gate. Tak, you keep them from getting onto the ship. Markus, you get us into the air."

"You got it, Captain."

Tak secured himself to the wall with a strap by the open gate and started closing it as Markus ran to the bridge. I stood back with Tak because I wasn't going to put one of my crew in danger without being there myself. The transport stopped and three men jumped out. One started shooting while two ran toward the spaceship. Tak shot back, but one of the two were able to jump on the closing gate. We were rising fast, and the gate was closing.

"Let go now or you are going to die," I yelled at the Tritonian who was climbing the gate. He either didn't hear me or was dead set on taking over the ship. He had dropped his gun to hold on with both hands, so I waited until the door closed. After it closed, I walked down to him, and grabbed him by the collar of his shirt, standing him up before I slammed him against the wall.

"Did you think you were... what? Going to take my ship?"

The Tritonian looked up at me, and I swore his blue skin paled when he saw me. "Please don't kill me. I was told there would only be two people on the ship, and it would be an easy score. Between the ship and the goods you're carrying, my boss could turn it around and give us all a good cut."

"Who's your boss? Why did he think I'd be a good score?"

"My boss is the arms runner who hired you. I don't know what name he used with you, but he said it was a quick run in and out with both loads and the ship."

"Oh, really? Tak, you stay with him, don't let him out of your sight. I'm going to have a conversation with Markus."

"Sure thing, Captain."

I turned to walk up to the bridge. Markus and I were going to have a talk before we decided what to do with our guest.

"Apparently, the client who had us come all the way out here wanted to leave us stranded."

Markus didn't look up from the controls. "And you found this out how?"

"We have a guest who jumped on board while you were lifting off."

"Isn't that something? Not something I would do, but there are some dumb people out there."

"Yes, there are, Markus. Yes, there are. Anyway, what do you think we should do?"

"Well, this shipment is going to Titan so we can drop him off there. I would say call the space cops. But I don't know if this load is hot or not, so we should probably drop him off at the same time."

"Sounds good. I'll let him know he's going to take a little trip."

With Markus laughing, I walked back to storage to let him know he should get comfortable. As I came in, Tak still had the weapon trained on him while he sat there with his head in his hands.

"We have decided you are going to join us on our trip to Titan to drop this off. After, you and this load will no longer be our problem."

"Wait, you are going to leave me there? How am I supposed to get back to Triton?"

"Not my problem. Why don't you call your boss? Maybe he can spring for a trip back to your home, or not. Do I need Tak to stay here with you to make sure you don't try to take over my ship, or are you going to behave and enjoy the ride?"

"It isn't like there's much I can do, is there?"

"No there isn't, so you might as well get comfortable. Trip is about 48 hours. I'll have Tak bring you some food." I left him to consider his situation.

Once we landed on Titan, we delivered the shipment and the Tritonian. Thankfully, the money was on contract creation, not contract completion.

"Captain, we have the load for Europa, and everything is secure. Are you ready?" Markus pulled me from my memory.

"Yup, thinking about the last time we were here. Let's get this load dropped off so we can get to Io and have some down time."

"Sounds good to me. We will be lifting off in about ten minutes."

I sat in my chair on the bridge and watched Markus effortlessly lift-off and put in coordinates for Europa. I re-read the contract and information about this 'Tahva', Princess of the moon Io, next to rule. *Wonder why she needs a match making service?*

CHAPTER 8

The morning Jasper was set to arrive, I found myself oddly nervous. Marci helped me find an outfit fit for royalty without being too ostentatious. The ride to the spaceport with Marci by my side did nothing to calm my nerves, and if anything, made it all the more real. I found myself looking around nervously as I waited at the space docks for this 'Jasper' guy.

"Princess, please stop pacing. You should sit down. We don't know how long it will be until he arrives. The notice said they had a few stops before this, so it may take a while."

"I can't, Marci. I know I should, but what if I'm not good enough? What if I'm ugly to him? I haven't been around many Humans."

"Seriously, the Princess of Io is worried about being pretty enough for some Human? Tahva, listen to me, we both know he'll find you beautiful. He'll be short, and you won't marry him. But until this pans out, can you please sit? You're making me nervous."

As I was moving to sit, I noticed a ship arriving.

When the small silver and blue ship landed, I was not impressed. Most ships arriving at this specific gate were much larger.

Apparently, Matching Galaxies doesn't have as much money as I thought they did.

When it rolled closer to the port, I read the name on the side, *'Stellar Kiwi'. What kind of name is 'Stellar Kiwi'?*

Even though I was nervous, I was going to have him meet me in my private room, not among the commoners. This was a Human. I know I could handle myself if he was here to hurt me. Not only was I likely taller than him, I had advanced hand to hand training.

As the loading gate lowered, I strained to see those getting off. First, what appeared to be a Titan walked up to one of the workers. No one else appeared for a bit, and suddenly, a smaller Human with brown hair walked down holding a clipboard. Knowing the man I'm supposed to meet is a captain, he wouldn't have a clipboard unless they did things differently on Earth. The next individual took my breath away. He was tall. From this angle, he looked to be almost my seven figs with bright red hair hanging in braids down his back. His skin was dark from either his ancestry or being in the sun. My mouth dried up. *This can't be him, but I want it to be.* I watched the men talk before the two Humans walked into the building.

"Your highness, there is a Jasper here to meet with you."

Daddy may have been right after all.

I stood and smoothed my gown. "You can let him in." I stood tall as my future 'husband' walked through the door.

***

The exchange of goods in Europa was a simple in and out. We took the resources from Triton and delivered them on schedule. The foreman of the project was glad to see us and mentioned something about how he wished all his deliveries were this on time and on price. It appeared they were having issues getting certain things. I told him while we had some other stops, if he wanted to get with Markus, we may be able to put a dent in of his needs. I didn't mention some of those supplies may not be procured legally. But the less the client knows, the better, especially when they think they're getting a great deal and on time. The crew and I made money, and we all knew what the consequences would be if we were ever caught.

"You ready to meet your future, Boss?" Markus joked as we were finalizing the shipment transfer and currency exchange.

"Keep your voice down. I don't want the crew to know."

"Calm down, if anyone was going to tell people, it would be my mom when she delivered those treats before she left, but even she didn't say anything. Your secret is safe with us."

"Wait, your mom brought treats? I didn't get any?"

"You are having an issue with not getting food? Focus Jasper."

"I am focused. Make sure the crew knows we're going to be on Io for a week. Markus, I want you to line up some more jobs, especially ones between Io and Earth."

"You want them above board?" Markus looked over the controls, preparing to leave.

"I don't care. All I ask is you make sure it's enough money to justify this jaunt out to Io."

"Will do, in the meantime, do you want to go tell the crew we have a week of R and R on Io?"

"What do you think I am? The captain or something?" I laughed as I headed back to the loading dock to let the rest of the crew know the next stop. To say they were excited to spend a week on Io was an understatement. Io was considered one of the party moons of the solar system due to their longer nights than days, drinking, partying, and other activities well known throughout the solar system. I knew my crew was going to be partying the entire time. I also knew them well enough to trust that the minute they were back on the ship, they would be sober and ready to work. One of many things I appreciated about my crew.

When we arrived, I instructed Markus to navigate away from all the hangars. "Land near the large building in front of us." A four-story building towered over the much smaller hangars, looking out of place at the airport. Looking through the windows, I could see what I thought was a woman standing in the window watching the ship come in. I couldn't see any details about her other than she was tall... or at least appeared tall. I didn't have a preference on how tall the women I dated where, but being close to seven foot myself, I did like taller women. I liked to dance, and dancing with girls on Earth who were under six feet was always awkward.

I left my bag on board because we would need to move the ship before the rest of the crew could leave. I also wanted to get this over with. Hopefully, after a week of spending time with me, the princess would decide she doesn't want to marry me. I had looked into Matching Galaxies, and their success rate was almost 100%. I don't know if I want to get married, but there was a level of excitement to this whole thing. I get to meet, and possibly marry, a real-life princess.

Markus walked into the building with me after talking to one of the port managers. He needed to check in with the main desk about where to store the ship for the duration of our trip.

Looking at the letter I'd received, I reread the directions. "Go to elevator B, press the crown. When you arrive, announce yourself, and you will meet Tahva." It seemed like a little much, but I'd signed the agreement stating I would go through with this. Finding the elevator, I pressed the button and was taken to a posh blue room with windows covered in flowers.

A Ioian man stood by the door and looked me over. He was my height with silver skin and pastel blue hair. With what appeared to be disgust, he raised his chin.

Don't take offense, get in and out.

"Hello, I'm Captain Jasper Moriarty. I'm here to see Tahva."

A brief look of shock passed over his face before it became neutral again. "Very well, let me make sure she is accepting guests as I was not informed."

What kind of princess has an announcer? To be fair, I don't know much royalty, but this seems over the top.

"Sir, she is ready to greet you. Please follow me."

As I walked through the door, I was immediately drawn to the striking woman in front of me. She was a little taller than me, which is normal for an Ioian, her skin was so silver I swore it was reflective. Her bright eyes seemed to see into my soul without trying. I was mesmerized until I heard a throat clear.

"Marci, please don't be rude."

I noticed another Ioian standing to the side of the princess.

"I'm sorry Ma'am. I really didn't like the way he was standing there staring at you without properly greeting you."

Great first impression, Jasper.

"It's nice to make your acquaintance, my lady." I bowed slightly, knowing royalty from other places liked such formalities. A small grin passed over Tahva's face before she became serious.

"Mr. Moriarty, may I speak with you alone?"

The announcer looked shocked again and stepped up as if he was going to say something.

"Deeth, stop right there, I'm safe with Mr. Moriarty. Please see Marci to the dining room."

With a nod, Deeth turned toward the door, expecting Marci to follow him. A single look back from the retreating Marci spoke volumes on how I shouldn't screw this up and what she thought of me.

"Now we're alone, Your Majesty. What do you want?"

CHAPTER 9

"I don't know your deal, or why you went to a matchmaking service, but here is why I went. I need to know something before I tell you."

"Okay?" Jasper asked.

"Can I trust you?"

"Princess, I don't know if you looked into me, but I'm one of the most trustworthy individuals you will ever meet. I run a business, own my own spaceship, and have my own crew."

"Yes, I know all about your 'business', both the legal and illegal sides. I also know about your crew and when you were almost space-jacked on Triton."

"Calm down with the 'almost space-jacked'. We had it under control the entire time. Also how did you know of our incident? No one mentioned it."

"Jasper, I have all the resources of the moon at my fingertips, and when I look into someone who may become my *husband,* I intend to find out everything I can."

"Fair, I admit I don't know much about you other than you are the princess of a moon."

"I expect not, with Earth's technology being what it is."

"I have all the newest and best technology in the solar system in my spaceship, so please stop with this 'I'm better than you' attitude and get down to what you want to tell me. I have a week before I leave."

"Wait, a week? A week isn't long enough to find out if we're compatible to marry or not. Why only a week? I wasn't informed."

The last bit was something of a screech. This was not going according to plan.

"Yes. You heard it right. You have a week before I leave again with my crew. We have jobs needing to be done. Not all of us were born into wealth."

"What did you say to me? I have things to do, too. My life isn't just about partying." I was furious. Why was this Human man talking to me like this?

"That isn't what I read."

I almost slapped him. So, he had looked into me. And to think I used to love the news circuits and their imagers.

Jasper took a step back. "I'm sorry. Please excuse my attitude. It was a long flight following a tense drop off in Triton. Please continue with what you were going to tell me."

I took a deep breath before I spoke. "I'm sorry as well. With my father being hurt and leaving unexpectedly without telling me where he was going, I've also been under a large amount of stress. I want to tell you about the current situation. But I needed to know I can trust you because I'm literally putting my father's life in your hands."

"You can trust me, but I'm unsure how your father's life is in my hands. I've never even met the man."

"Regardless of how we feel about each other, we must marry within the next three months. So, this will be a business arrangement."

I spelled out exactly why I need to get married and my stipulations. Through the whole thing, Jasper stood there with his hands clasped behind his back. I couldn't even tell what he was thinking, and usually I can with most people. "Well, do you have anything to say?"

"It seems like you have a lot going on. My deal is much simpler. You meet my sister and her daughters. If they decide they want to, they may come and stay with us. Otherwise, I'm a transporter, so I won't be here all the time, and I'm independent. If you're good with what we've discussed, let's make this a business arrangement."

"Let's cut to the chase, you're a pirate, and a good one from what I can find. I'm a party girl who likes to dance. We're the same but different. While I'm not a huge fan of kids, being an only child, my house is big enough to accommodate them. What are their names?"

Jasper chuckled. "My sister is Jasmine. She's younger than me. Her daughters are Jannie which stands for Janella. The youngest is Julianne, but when Jannie was younger, she couldn't pronounce it, so she started calling her Juju, and it stuck."

"Interesting, well if you're in agreement, let's go back to the mansion so I can show you where you'll be staying. You said your crew is staying as well, will they also need accommodations?"

"While thoughtful, no. They'll either be staying on the ship or in someone's bed. They don't get downtime often. But thank you for the offer"

"I can imagine. Well, let's get back to the mansion."

"Sounds good to me, Princess."

I enjoyed how princess rolled off his tongue with his Human accent.

***

Walking behind the princess, I was suddenly not as confident as I had been when I'd agreed to this business arrangement. Jasmine and my parent's love survived through everything. Their love was something Jasmine and I always wanted growing up. Jasmine had gotten her love until a rogue ship had fired on the Rio, taking her husband and the girl's dad away from them. *No, I'll do it. If nothing else than to provide a safe location for my crew when we need to lay low.* The more I think about it, the more I'm certain this is the best option, at least for right now.

We walked outside the building, and there was a car waiting for Tahva and me. We rode in silence, but it wasn't awkward, in fact, it was a nice kind of quiet. I usually feel the need to engage in conversation, especially with everything going on, but I didn't feel the need this time. The ride didn't seem long and before I knew it, we were turning into a circular driveway.

As we pulled up to the house, I heard an 'oohh' and 'ahh', and realized it was coming from me. It was a spectacular building. It looked to be built from stone.

"What is this building made of? It's beautiful, but I've never seen such a stone."

"It's built with stone from asteroids mined when Io's capital city was being built. This is the oldest building aside from some of the old mining buildings near what is now the spaceport. You know, until now, it's been home. I've never looked at it as anything other than a building holding the power of the royal family."

"It's a magnificent building." I turned to look back at the vehicle as we arrived at the door.

Three stone stairs led to a red, wooden double door with glazed glass panes. One pane of glass depicted the solar system, and the other was a crest of some sort. The crest was divided into four parts, and the top left section was a crown with thorns. The top right section was Jupiter, the planet Io orbits. The lower left section contained a large X, and the lower right section showed a red and white flower similar to Earth's manuka, a flower which blooms in New Zealand.

"Is this your family's crest?" I held the door open for Tahva before we walked up the steps.

"Yes, the X is for my family's last name. The flower is a flower my mother loved and planted in various places throughout the house. Jupiter is for the planet giving us life, or at least the one we orbit. The crown with thorns is our royalty, but with power comes pain, and with control comes hard decisions."

I didn't know what to say. My family had never had a crest, at least as far as I knew of. It was both beautiful and powerful, the fragility of the flower with the power of the crown.

"Thank you for explaining it to me. What's next?"

"When we get inside, I'll have Marci show you to your room so you can rest if you want."

"Princess, what do you intend to do?" I asked.

"While I like hearing you call me princess, can you please call me Tahva, especially since I'll be a queen soon?"

I smiled at her. I realized I was getting under her skin.

"Since my recent birthday was ruined by all this, I was thinking about going to the club. Tomorrow, I can show you the property and the moon if you want. Since you'll be here for at least a week, you should get to know the area. Right now, though, I'm going to go to my father's office and to get some food and get changed. Do you want to join me?"

I didn't expect her to be so forward, so I blushed a little at her words.

She must have realized what she had said because she quickly followed up with, "I meant to the office and to get food, I prefer to change alone."

"Of course I would, considering I'm to be your consort."

She led the way to the office, pausing to open a panel on the side of the door before tapping a series of numbers. As I entered, I looked at the bookcases full of books. A large desk sat in front of a large window. Walking over to the window, I noticed a large flower garden along with a walking path outside. The flowers in the garden matched those of the door.

"This is the king's office?"

"Yes, well technically, I guess it will be the queen's office soon. What do you want to eat? I'll have the chef bring us something here so I can draft the letter to be delivered to the council showing our intent to marry. I plan on still being asleep when they respond, but this needs to be submitted. I can imagine they're in a tizzy thinking they can control me or the throne."

While I thought about what I wanted to eat, I watched Tahva drafting the letter explaining how we had met and notifying them we plan to marry.

The smirk on Tahva's face while she wrote must mean she was enjoying the letter she was writing.

"I'd like to try something native, or whatever you're having Prin... I mean, Tahva."

"Let's eat something quick so I can get to the club."

"You mean *we're* going to the club, right?"

"Absolutely not. I'm going to go and enjoy my time, alone. You can stay here, I can have Marci take you around the moon to do some sightseeing, or you can go back to your ship, but I'm going by myself.

***

Who does he think he is demanding he come with me? Maybe this wasn't such a good idea after all.

I'm not some fragile flower, and if I want to go to the club by myself, I'll go to the club myself. No one, not even my father, told me what to do or when to do it. Why should this man, who thinks he's going to be my husband, come in here thinking he's some kind of knight? If I wanted a knight, I would hire one.

If he was going to insist on going with me, I was going to make him regret it. As I looked over my wardrobe, I picked an outfit I knew he would drool over. Pulling the dress and shoes from my closet, I put them on the bed before walking into the bathroom to shower.

As I washed my hair, I thought about Jasper. He was quiet, but also strong. I still didn't believe I needed someone by my side, but if Jasper was the one I was forced to be with, I guess there were worse choices.

"Well Mom, I know it isn't the same as you and dad, but I hope it works out. I need it to." As I dressed, I talked to my mother's image, a constant reminder of what I had lost. *Maybe if she was still around, I wouldn't be in this position.* There was nothing I could do about it. She had been gone for years, and no matter how much I wished for it, she wasn't coming back. Now I need to step it up, become queen, and bring my father home.

***

62

What is it with me and hard-headed women?

When I finished eating, I went up to the room Tahva had said was mine. It was in the same wing as hers. While I waited for Tahva to get dressed, I wandered through the house. I could hear Marci talking to someone I assumed was the chef. I walked out the back entry way onto a stone patio overlooking the same garden I'd seen from the king's office. Turning, I saw the windows to that room.

As I made my way back to the staircase, I turned to see Tahva at the top. She was breathtaking in a green mini-dress and black gladiator heels. I watched as she descended.

"You look amazing."

"Thank you, but you're still not going with me." Tahva tucked her clutch under her arm as she took my outstretched hand with her other.

"You're welcome, and yes, I am. Listen, I talked to Marci about your father. I think it would be best if you had someone with you, in case something happens tonight. Especially since no one knows about me here yet other than Marci, you, and my crew. I don't want to take the chance of anything to happen to you."

It was true. I wanted to get to know her, even if our marriage doesn't end up lasting. Assuming we even get married in the first place.

"Under one condition." I swore I saw Tahva preen as she spoke.

"Which is?" She was going to keep me on my toes, I knew it.

"You can't be near me all the time. You have to let me dance and enjoy myself. Soon, I'll have to take on a lot of responsibility, and I want is this one small thing."

"Fine, but under one of my conditions." I watched her deflate, but she rolled her shoulders back.

"Which is?"

"If I tell you we must go, or if I tell you to drop, you do it. No hesitation, no questions. Do you understand me?"

"I'll agree to your conditions, but you better not be doing it because you're tired."

"I've have stayed up for over fifty hours straight before while being chased, I think I can manage to keep up with some dancing."

"We shall see." Tahva moved past me to the front door, letting it slide open. She stood in the doorway. "Are you coming?"

She lifted a perfectly manicured eyebrow, and I felt myself following her like an Earth dog.

What have I gotten myself into?

***

The music made me forget everything else currently happening in my life. The impending marriage, the family I was going to be part of if I married this man, my father being gone, becoming queen soon, everything. I wasn't ready. I don't even know if this is what I want. Oh Jupiter, Jasper was attractive, but could he keep up with me? I didn't need him to make me happy, I can do that myself. But if I was going to marry, I expect him to heel to me, not the other way around. I also knew I was born ready. My parents only ever wanted one child, so I was destined to rule from the beginning. I never thought I would rule with a Human beside me, but for Humans, he wasn't bad. Much better than those who flock around the regency council.

I caught myself glancing over at Jasper, who was positioned by the bar. I realized he could see everything from there, from me dancing to who was coming into the club or leaving. I made sure the owners knew how to take good care of him, telling them he was my stand-in bodyguard because Roald was on an important trip. I chuckled when a Titanian tried to flirt with him. Her black hair reminded me of someone. I wanted to tell her he was hands-off, but before I could, she left on her own with a look of rejection. *Maybe I don't have to worry about Jasper after all.* I was used to men who, while out with me, were looking for their next conquest, and it was tiresome. Maybe I did want someone who wanted to be with me for who I am, not for the power my family wielded.

As I was thinking about Jasper, I heard one of my favorite songs start pumping through the speakers. I jumped up and down and moved closer to the DJ. My body moved to the music, and it felt like I was going into the trance I sometimes go into while dancing. Roald used to say it could be hours before my eyes unglazed. *I'm going to miss these days. Maybe I could build a club somewhere I could go to. I could even take Jasper's sister. I wonder if she likes to dance?*

Suddenly, I heard a voice yell 'down' right as someone pushed me to the ground. I felt a burning sensation on my shoulder. I was mad at first, but my brain recognized the voice was Jasper's, and I looked for him. Standing, I looked for his red hair, and I saw him near the bar talking to one of the owners. Looking at my shoulder, I realized I had some sort of burn there. *How did that happen? I'm going to talk to the owner myself.* When I approached the bar, the owner ran over and hugged me.

"I'm so glad you're okay. If it wasn't for Jasper, I don't know what would have happened."

"What do you mean you're glad I'm okay? What happened?"

***

Watching Tahva dance was intoxicating. Her body flowed and moved with the music in ways I'd never seen before. I wasn't a frequent club goer, but some of the crew were, and we had

65

protection details before. I was well acquainted with how clubs could be. In fact, I saw Markus over along the wall flirting with a Martian.

He saw me and nodded before going back to talking to the young lady.

I'm glad at least a few of my crew members are enjoying the liberty leave. The line of thinking led me to what I was planning to do with my ship and my crew if the situation with Tahva works out. I didn't want to give up everything, and I wasn't willing to leave the guys stranded. They were a good crew and deserved the work.

While I was looking over the club, I noticed a Titanian who didn't appear to be interested in dancing. Instead, he was focused on one specific dancer, Tahva. Thinking maybe it was someone she knew, I watched a bit longer before he looked around. He appeared to be making sure no one was watching him.

Right as I moved closer to Tahva, the hairs on the back of my neck tingled.

"Does the Titanian over there have a gun?" Markus asked as he slid up next to me.

"I don't know but I don't like it. I'll go check him out. See the tall Ioian with the green dress dancing like she owns the club? Get near her. If I yell down, you pull her down as fast and hard as you can."

"I'm not even going to ask. You know I'll got it." Markus started toward Tahva.

When I noticed Markus in position close to Tahva, I walked up to the man as he pulled the weapon from under his jacket. *How was he allowed in the club with the weapon?* When Tahva and I had arrived, I noticed a multi-stage procedure ensuring no weapons were allowed in. Unless, of course, the stranger had someone to help him bypass security like Tahva had done. *Must be nice to be royalty.*

As he took aim at Tahva, I yelled "DOWN!", I saw the weapon go off as Markus pushed her down. I went to grab the shooter, but he slipped between some dancers who hadn't noticed the commotion. In an instant, I saw him run out a door leading to what I knew was the main transport road. Instead of chasing him, I went to the bar where one of the owners stood.

"Did you see a Titanian run through here?"

"No, what happened? Do I need the bouncers to come get him?"

"No use, he's already gone. He tried to kill Tahva. How did he get in here with a weapon?" I usually didn't demand things from people I barely knew. This was the soon to be queen and possibly my wife's life. Regardless, I was going to protect her while I could, even if that wasn't for long.

"What? No way, are you sure?"

Tahva stormed up with Markus following a short distance behind. The owner ran up and hugged her while Markus sidestepped them and walked over to me.

"Did you get him?"

"No, but I need you to do something for me. I want to know if there's any scuttle on the circuit. This was a Titanian, and he was aiming for her. I need you to do it on the sly."

"If you trust him, I'll give him access to the royal resources. No one tries to hurt me without severe consequences." Tahva stood right in front of me with her hands on her hips.

"Markus, it looks like you're coming to the royal mansion."

Markus arched his brow and looked between us but didn't ask any questions. I could tell he had them, but he wasn't going to ask right now.

"Sounds good, should I grab my bag from the ship?"

"No, I want you to come with us now to the mansion and start investigating this individual."

"Markus, please let me introduce you to Tahva, Princess of Io. Tahva, this is my second in command, Markus."

"I would say it's a pleasure to meet you but given the circumstances...."

"It will be a pleasure if you can find out who attacked me. If you think you can, anyway."

"Ma'am, I could find a pin in a haystack. I think I can find a Titan on Io, as long as I can get footage of the individual from the club."

Tahva turned to the owners. "You will get this man what he wants, correct?"

The owners bowed their head slightly before one of them responded, "Anything to ensure your safety."

***

"No one was trying to kill me. I got burned by one of the falling sparklers the DJ used."

"Tahva, for the last time, I know what I saw. The owner is going through the images now to see how he got in with a weapon. We need to go back to the mansion."

As much as I didn't want to, I knew with tomorrow being the day I was supposed to start digging into becoming a queen, Jasper was right. I looked at my shoulder. It was healing slowly, and thankfully whoever tried to hurt me didn't damage my dress. I could still wear it again. I slid into the backseat of the Limber while Jasper sat next to me, and Markus sat in front. Still pouting, I spit, "Fine, but I don't like it."

When we arrived at the mansion, Jasper opened the door for me. "I'll take what I can get, but please be safe. We need to get Markus set up with access to security, and I'll be outside your door all night, so if you need anything please let me know."

His words made my heartbeat faster. *It was from the fact he saved me, not anything else,* I told myself.

"There's no need for all that; this place is secure," I spoke over my shoulder as I walked to the office. The sooner I get Markus set up, the sooner I can get to my room and think about what had happened earlier.

As I walked into the office, I went straight to the desk to open the circuit for Markus. "Do you know how to use this?"

"I do. I'm well versed in this type of device. We have a similar one on the ship. Are you sure it's secure?"

"Yes, no one will be able to see what you're doing, and you have full access to whatever you need. Do not make me regret using my royal access codes."

"I'll do my best to ensure nothing illegal is done." Markus sat in front of the device.

Jasper put his hand on the small of my back. "It's time for you to go to your room. If you need anything, please let me know, and I'll have Marci bring it up."

As much as I wanted to step away from his hand, being the independent future Queen of Io, it felt nice on my back. "Like I said before, this place is secure."

"I'll be the judge of that." He kept his hand on my back while we walked up the stairs. It felt safe, like I was protected. My entire life I knew I was protected because of who I am, but this was the first night I actually felt protected. As we reached my room, Jasper opened the door for me before saying goodnight. I shut my door, leaning against it. I did feel safer with him being on the other side of the door, but I wasn't going to admit it to him. I didn't know if I wanted to admit it to myself, but this man was starting to break through my defenses.

CHAPTER 10

As I told Tahva I would, I stood outside her door the entire night, only leaving one time to call Jasmine to check on her and the girls. While on the intercell waiting for Jasmine to answer, I walked down to the office. Since Tahva hadn't given me the passcode to the door, I knocked, hoping Markus didn't have his earplugs in. Sometimes when he was working hard, he would put in earplugs, so nothing broke his concentration. Markus opened the office door at the same time Jasmine answered the intercell.

Without saying anything to Markus, I walked over to the desk with him. Jasmine showed me an image of the girls completely lost in the big bed they shared; the only thing visible was their red hair peeking out from under the blankets. Jasmine was up checking on the pets and was about to go to sleep when I called.

"Things here are quiet; how are things there? How's Tahva?"

Not wanting to worry her about what had happened at the club, I changed the subject. "Things are good. Tahva is beautiful, a real princess. She's a little taller than me."

"How long do you plan on staying on Io, and is Markus near you?"

I turned the screen to Markus so he could wave to Jasmine before going back to the computer.

"I plan on being here for about a week before we ship out for the rest of our contracts. Markus needed to do some research on a job we have coming up, so Tahva was nice enough to let him use her system versus having to go back to the ship."

If Jasmine knew something was up, she didn't let on. We spoke for for a little longer, she said her goodnights, and we hung up.

"Have you found anything yet?"

"I have a string I'm pulling at, and the owners of the club were fast about getting the footage back to us. A plus, I guess."

"Tahva has a lot of pull, but she doesn't seem to use it much."

"I don't know. From what I've seen, she seems a bit of a prima donna. She's an only child, isn't she?"

"She's definitely a prima donna, and yeah, she is. How'd you know?"

"I guessed by the way she stormed up to the owners at the club after she got hurt. Is she alright?"

"Yeah, I think she's alright, at least physically. The Ioians have healing properties, so they tend to be able to heal from much more serious wounds, and a lot more quickly than we do."

"What's going on with you two?"

Sitting in a chair across from Markus, I thought before I answered.

"I don't know, Markus. Right now, it's a business arrangement. She needs a consort in order to become queen, and we matched."

"Boss, we've known each other a long time. You don't seem to be a 'business arrangement' of a wedding type of person."

"I'm not normally. There's something about her I'm intrigued by, but I don't know if I can be a princess's, or queen's, consort and still travel the way we do. I can't sit back and never fly again."

Markus nodded in understanding.

For as long as I've known him, we both needed to fly, to get off Earth and explore. I always figured we would be exploring and working together for the rest of our lives, or until something happened, forcing us to quit. *Was this something worth quitting for?*

"Boss, it's not something you need to decide right now. Let's figure out who tried to hurt her, get back out there for our contracts, and we can work from there."

"Look at you, always thinking ahead. If you need anything, I'll be back in front of Tahva's door. I want to be there when she wakes up. I have a feeling there's more going on with this Titanian than some random guy trying to hurt her."

"I'm glad you said something, because I feel the same way. It was too coincidental. The same day she returned to the club, there so happens to be someone there to hurt her? It doesn't add up."

I told Markus I would see him later and left. My thoughts turned to what had happened and the reasons why. I didn't want to think whoever was going after Tahva's father could now be after her, but it seemed to fit too well for it not to be connected. I stood in front of her door thinking about my life and how my future could be changed forever.

The next morning when Tahva opened her door, I was standing in front of it, as I told her I would. I was getting close to my limit on staying awake, though. She smiled before letting me know she was going to clean up and would be ready for breakfast in 10 minutes. In exactly 10, she was back at the door wearing a flowing dress and sandals.

"Ready?"

"For breakfast? Yes, I'm starving. Healing causes me to need more food."

"To show me around, not to eat."

"I'll have to change again before we leave, but yes, I think I am."

I reached out to take her hand as we moved to the dining room. "Shall we go, then?"

Scoffing while also smiling, Tahva took my hand. "We shall."

We walked into the dining room, already a frenzy of activity with Markus eating and Marci making sure he had everything he needed.

Everyone stopped their activity and watched as we walked in. Markus stood, and Marci walked over to the princess before Tahva held up her hand.

"No need, Marci. Please get Jasper whatever he wants and get me my regular breakfast."

Tahva and I sat near Markus.

"Thank you, Marci. Can I please have whatever you've brought Markus?"

Marci nodded before returning to the kitchen.

"What's the plan for today?" Markus asked between mouthfuls of food.

"Well, for you to not choke yourself while eating is a priority."

"Haha." Markus threw a napkin at me.

"Yeah Markus, please don't choke," Tahva chimed in with a small laugh. As the words left her mouth, Marci returned with a small cart of food.

"Actually, Tahva is planning on showing me around the moon and the house today. Have you found out anything from the circuit?"

Marci placed the food in front of Tahva and I, and we ate in silence while Markus finished his food.

"I found the guy, but it won't help."

"Why won't it help? Can't we simply find him and question why he did what he did?"

"If you can bring a Titan back from the dead, then yes, we can question him."

"Markus, we saw him last night. What are you talking about he's dead?"

"Well two-fold, technically, since he's died twice."

"Markus, less riddles, and more answers please." I swore Markus's favorite way to mess with me was to give me the bare minimum of information. He did it on contracts sometimes, too. I knew he would never put the crew or ship in danger, but pulling information from him could be tiring to say the least.

"The guy who shot at Tahva last night died two years ago, allegedly. Or at least the Titan with the name he was using when he landed on Io died."

A heavy sigh could be heard as Tahva sank a little in her seat. "So, we have no idea who it was?"

"Give me a little credit. The Titanian who was on Io last night arrived with a fake name. Soon after he left the club, he was seen near the spaceport trying to catch a flight back to Titan."

I could tell Markus had found something by the way his speech sped up. Whatever he found, he was excited.

"Did he leave the moon?"

"No, he didn't. He tried to get on a ship, but there weren't any going to Titan, only to Europa with building materials. There was one leaving this morning, so he decided he was going to wait in the spaceport lobby and catch the flight. This was all about three hours after he shot you. You don't look like you were injured."

"More information, less chit chat." I love Markus like a brother, but sometimes he got derailed from what he should be discussing.

"Okay, okay. He went into the spaceport lobby to wait for the flight to Titan. After 30 minutes, he received an intercell call. He took the call, walking outside where a black car was waiting. As he went to open the back door of the vehicle to get in, he was shot. Two men came out of a hangar and picked up his body. From there, they carried it back into the hanger. About twenty minutes later, a small plane took off from the hangar. I followed the path of the plane and caught it dropping something over a lake. I'm guessing his body will be found in the lake."

"What lake was it?"

Markus checked his intercell where he kept all his notes in case any questions were asked that he didn't have the answer for.

"It looks like the name of it is Loki Patera."

"That's what I thought. Loki Patera is a lava lake, so there won't be any remnants left if the body has been in there for more than an hour."

"Wow, Boss, it would be nice if we had a lava lake to help with some of our jobs."

I could tell Markus was already thinking about the benefits of having a lake to destroy evidence.

"Markus, you're saying you found all this information in less than a day? I should hire you myself."

"Sorry Ma'am, but at least for right now, I have a good paying job." Markus smiled as Marci put more food in front of him.

Way to rub it in regarding the ship. Did he actually think I would leave him abandoned?

"If you ever decide you'd like a part-time job when you're on Io, please let me know."

"Thank you, Tahva. I'll definitely keep it in mind."

Yeah, I'm sure you will.

***

What have I gotten myself into? Possibly marrying a stranger soon after meeting him? Having an instant family? What would Mother say?

Looking at the image of her, I knew exactly what she would say.

"Honey, you're doing what you feel is right. Keep following your head and your heart, and you'll never go wrong."

It was something she'd told me frequently growing up, especially when I was struggling with a decision.

Keep the course. It'll all work out in the end.

Marci arrived to help me pick which dress and jewelry to wear. I still missed Roald but felt safe with Jasper. Without Marci, I'd be completely lost. I had no idea what I should wear to show my potential consort the moon. There will be individuals from the circuit waiting to take my image. The constantly partying princess was settling down; I could see the headlines now. In no time, I was dressed in a royal blue pantsuit with my mother's casual jewelry. I realized this was the first time I'd worn her jewels. Looking in the mirror, I didn't recognize the Ioian looking back at me. I was no longer the little girl playing dress-up in her mother's clothes. I was now the princess who was all grown up and about to take the next step in life. Whatever it meant, marriage or not, I was moving into a new stage, and I didn't know if I was ready for it.

"Are you ready?" Marci asked as I turned away from the mirror.

"As ready as I'll ever be." With a small smile, I walked to the door as a knock sounded.

Opening the door, I saw Jasper in a gray tailored suit.

I wonder where he got it from. You don't see many pirates having the need for such a nice suit. He does look good in it, though.

"You know you don't have to dress up, right? We're going around the moon and meeting a few people."

"I wasn't going to wear my flight suit or the clothes I wore last night. You and I both know there will be imagers, and I want to make sure I look good on your arm."

Who is this man who seems to care as much about me as he does himself?

***

When the door opened, I stood speechless. I'd seen Tahva dressed up before, but this was a level of regal I wasn't ready for. The jewelry on her throat glinted under the hallway lights.

Holding my arm out, she took it with a tight grip.

"Nervous?"

Tahva spoke softly so only I could hear, "A little, this obviously isn't the first time I've been out on the moon with a man, but you aren't just anyone. And what if the man who tried to hurt me last night was hired by someone who is adamant about finishing the job?"

"Two things, this is your home, your moon, and we will control things as we travel around. If you're uncomfortable, all you have to do is squeeze my hand, and I'll get you out of any situation. An assassin would have to have a death wish to try attacking you in front of all the imagers following us as we tour the moon. Also, I have Markus working on a schedule with Marci, so he knows where you'll be taking me. At no time will we be without one of my crew near us. I trust them with my life. How do you feel now?"

Tahva leaned into my shoulder. "I'm grateful the matchmaking service found you."

I could get used to her resting her head on my shoulder like this. It feels natural.

"I am too. Are you ready to get the tour started?"

"As ready as I think I'll ever be. I don't know why I'm so nervous all of a sudden."

"I'm nervous too. We'll get through it together."

***

Without thinking, I held Jasper's hand as we walked out to the vehicle. I was surprised by how nervous I was to show him around. I wanted him to like it and to see the moon for all its good things.

What am I even talking about? Why do I care if he likes the moon? Oh yeah, that's right, because I have to marry in order to become queen.

"Where are we off to first?" Jasper asked as we got into the transport. I had decided not to take the Limber because it was too flashy for what I wanted to do today. If anything, I would like to show Jasper the moon without any of the circuits finding us. I made sure to silence my intercell so if it was an emergency they could still get through, but it wouldn't actively disturb us.

"I was thinking of first going through the towns and different spaceports before I show you the outskirts and the rural areas." I wanted to the end the tour at a specific place. I hoped Jasper liked it.

As we traveled through the capital city of Io, I pointed out buildings of interest. I felt like a tour guide, but I was glad I'd listened as a child and growing up. I could talk about the history of the city, as well as the moon, without having to consult the on board comm device.

"What's that building?" Jasper pointed at a purple building situated in the middle of a park.

"It's the office of the regency council."

"I thought Io was controlled by royalty?"

Turning so I could see Jasper's face, I took a deep breath before explaining, "Yes, Io is controlled by the Xi family. The regency council is a cross between a business' board of directors and an advice group."

"So, they are something of a balance to the sole leader?"

Cute and smart. I should send Matching Galaxies a gift basket for matching me with Jasper.

"Exactly. They can't change anything, but they work with the royal family to take on some of the more mundane tasks so the royal family can focus on more important matters."

Jasper nodded as I spoke.

"That makes sense. On Earth, we have various governments in different locations, and while there are some like what you have here, we also have some which are totally different. We have governments completely elected by the citizens of the region they serve. Sadly, other place's officials are not elected but have complete and total control over their region without the citizens having a say."

"Sadly?" I folded my arms across my chest.

"In some cases, people who aren't elected don't look out for the best interests of their citizens," Jasper replied. "I wasn't talking about you."

"Does having different types of governments ever cause issues?" I never thought about planets or other moons and how they survive. I realized I've been self-centered about my own wants and needs and didn't think about what could happen with my people when I took the throne. I knew my father interacted with governments from all over the solar system. Maybe there was a small part of me which thought my father would always be the king, so why worry about what happened outside of my own little sphere.

"All the time. You have some governments who want more land, some who are only trying to survive, and others who want more power. Sadly, it's never ending in some parts of Earth. You would think after centuries of fighting, there'd be a time when the fighting would stop. But so far it hasn't, and that's how Jasmine and I lost our parents."

I reached over and grasped Jasper's hand. I could tell fighting was hard for him to talk about. "Tell me more about your parents?" I could tell he loved them deeply by the way his eyes misted over.

"They were great. My parents were born and raised on New Zealand, an island in the Pacific Ocean, which is the largest body of water on Earth. My mother was a doctor who specialized in helping burn victims. Unlike Ioians, we don't heal as fast as you do, so doctors are needed throughout our entire lifetime. My father was a government official and a part time military officer. They were dedicated to ending war, but when one of our allies was being invaded by another country, they were called to help. Because of who they were, they answered the call to help those in need. Jasmine and I were young, and it's how I met Markus. When our parents left, we were sent to Australia to live with a friend of theirs until they returned. They were neighbors of Markus and his mom, Cynthia. Markus' father also served as an officer. He oversaw intelligence, so he worked closely with both my mother and father." Jasper paused and took a hitched breath.

I slid closer to him and put my hand on his thigh.

"It's alright. We don't have to talk about it."

"No, I want to. I don't talk about them enough. They would have liked you so much, especially my mother. She was strong, fearless, and so protective of not just Jasmine and me, but for those who she helped heal."

"I'm sure she and your father would be very proud of the man you've become."

Jasper chuckled. "Well, maybe not totally who I am, since what I do isn't always legal, but I do try to help people when I can, and we were able to keep the property we grew up on. Anyway, they were on a base in another country, helping to slow the spread of war. The base was hit, even though it was in the middle of a town and shouldn't have been. The attacker said it was a mistake, but the mistake killed ten people, including my parents, Markus' father, four patients my mom was helping, and three other soldiers from Australia."

"Jasper, I'm so sorry. Is that why you and Markus work together?"

"Yes and no. Jasmine and I lived with my parent's friends until we graduated from school and moved back to the family home. I went to work while Jasmine went to further her education. While I was working, I realized I couldn't stay on Earth forever. Sooner or later another war would start, or something would happen to cause me to become involved, and I didn't want that. I saved my money and bought a spaceship. I learned how to fly, but realized I couldn't do it on my own. Markus was the first one I reached out to. He was also working, living with, and supporting his mother. He jumped at the opportunity for change, and together we went into business. We promised each other even though I owned the ship, everything was split with the crew. I never took more than them. Over time, we gathered a crew we all trusted with our lives, and let me tell you, there have been some situations where our trust has been put to the test. Enough about me. Tell me more about you and Io."

I could tell Jasper was remembering things he didn't want to and wanted to change the subject.

"Io has been peaceful since our creation. There is fighting sometimes, and we aren't necessarily a peaceful people, but with Io being so small, there aren't a lot of resources to fight over. Before we started to terraform the country, there were few habitable places, and so the population stayed small and tightknit. Recently, however, there has been more violence, specifically the spaceport or the outskirts. It's something my father and the regency council have been working on. Well, and terraforming Europa."

Jasper let go of my hand.

"Wait, Io is terraforming Europa? Are they working with Triton? Before meeting you, we were brought out this far for a job taking materials from Triton to Europa."

Considering what he had said, I thought about it. "I don't know the specifics. I do know my father and a council member recently fought about it. I do believe Io was working with other moons and planets on the project." Now I wish I'd listened more when my father had talked about it in the past.

"If you're interested, when we get back to the mansion, we can go through my father's comm device and see if there's anything on there about it. Do you think it has something to do with why I was attacked?"

Jasper looked deep in thought but didn't answer right away.

"Jasper. What are you thinking?"

"I don't know, but it seems like some loose ends may need to be tied up before you become queen."

***

I hadn't planned to talk about my parents with Tahva. It was always a hard topic for me. I was young, but Jasmine was even younger, and sometimes I worried she didn't remember them. After everything that happened with Raf's death, I wondered if her not remembering them was a kinder thing. Next time I see her, we should sit and talk about our parents. We didn't do nearly enough to keep their memories alive. It was always the kangaroo in the room, something we knew was there, but we never talked about them. I think it was a disservice to who they were and what they did to help others.

The information about Io terraforming Europa prompted my brain to try to remember something, but it was right on the edge of my memory. Sooner or later, I would remember. Hopefully it wasn't anything too important and right now, all I could think about was how close Tahva was and how her hand felt on my thigh.

We were outside of town and barely left the spaceport when Tahva mentioned she had a surprise for me. I was excited to see what she had in mind. In the week since we first met, she'd been standoffish and self-centered, but there seemed to be another side to her. As I considered her, my intercell rang. I forgot to mute it and was about to apologize for the disruption when I saw it was Cynthia, Markus' mother, calling me.

"Hi Cynthia, how's my favorite second mother?" My smile disappeared the moment she spoke.

"Jasper, you have to come home. Jasmine's missing." It sounded like Cynthia was hyperventilating.

"Slow down, what do you mean Jasmine's missing?"

I noticed Tahva sat up straighter and mouthed, 'Is everything okay?'

I shook my head as I listened.

"I got a call from Jannie, you know how I'm on the intercell as an emergency contact for the girls to call. She said she and juju were inside while Jasmine was outside tending to the animals when she said heard a whoosh and her mom scream. Jannie, you know how she is. She's fearless like her mom, so she went outside to see what was going on. She said Jasmine was being pulled into a spaceship that left in a hurry. Jannie made sure the animal pen was closed before she came in and called me. I came over immediately."

"She was taken? Why? She doesn't do anything other than raise animals and do science stuff. Poor Jannie, does Juju know? I'm coming home right now."

I could see Tahva was listening intently, while she was also messaging someone.

"Juju doesn't know what happened yet. Jannie's doing as well as can be expected, and I don't know, Jasper..." A sob came over the intercell.

I could tell Cynthia wasn't doing well. Who was I kidding? I wasn't either. No one takes my sister without serious consequences.

"Cynthia, I'm coming home. I'll have Markus get the ship ready. Will you be okay with the girls for the next week while we get back to Earth? Please take them back to your house with you."

"Absolutely not, Jasper. I'm not going to let the animals suffer or take the girls away from their home because of some criminal. I'll be here when you get back, but you'd better find them, and you'd better make them pay."

"I will, Cynthia. I promise I will. I'll see you soon." I hung up. I didn't know what to say or what to do. I couldn't think, I couldn't react, which wasn't normal for me. I was the captain of a ship which routinely outran both mercenaries and police alike, but now I was lost.

By the time I realized what was going on, we'd turned around and were back at the mansion.

"What are we doing back here? We have to —" I started, but Tahva stopped me.

⁎

The minute I heard Jasmine was gone, I knew I had to do something. I first told the driver to turn around and head back to the

86

mansion. I contacted Marci on my intercell to call Markus and let him know to get the ship ready. I also had Marci pack a bag for me and draft a letter to the regency council. I didn't even know if Jasper would be okay with what I had planned, but I had a feeling he needed me there.

"I turned the transport around, and Marci packed your stuff. She'll be out with the bags soon. Markus is already on the way to the ship to get it ready, and I contacted the spaceport's manager to let him know the Stellar Kiwi needed an expedited take-off on my orders."

"Wait, you did all those things while I was on the phone? Really, you did that for me?"

I held Jasper's hand. "Jasper, I know how much family means to you. I can hear it in your voice when you talk about them. I'm not going to tell you to not go to, and I'll help however I can."

I opened the transport door and stepped out. I moved to the side so Jasper could exit as well. He embraced me.

"Thank you so much, Tahva. I can't seem to think clearly, so I appreciate you taking care of everything like you did. What will you do while I'm gone?"

I wrapped my arms around him and took deep breaths. I felt at ease in his arms, even with everything going on.

The moment of truth.

"I'm going with you, and before you can stop me, please listen. We don't know if whoever tried to hurt me the other night will try again. What if it's connected to my or my father's attacks? I can ease the way with the solar police if we need it, and if the person or persons responsible for Jasmine's abduction is Ioian, I have the power to unilaterally punish them immediately."

"Absolutely not, you're a princess, and you need to stay here. Even though you make good points, I cannot allow you to be put into danger."

I stood there with one hand on my hip and tapping the toe of my shoe. "If you won't let me join as your intended wife to help what may be my future family, I'll charter your ship."

Jasper looked from my face, to my hand, and to my foot before looking back at my face. "You'll what? You can't come and charter my ship, especially since you know what I need to do. We don't have to accept every charter offer."

"You don't, but you're on Io land, and I'm a reigning royal. I can commandeer it if I want. I do know what you have to do. Go find your sister and protect you family, but I'm leaving with the ship either as a helper or as a client." I was going to be on the ship. I didn't understand this version of myself, though, or the words coming out of my mouth. I'd never left the moon, preferring to stay grounded versus being in space. My mom's advice for all those years kept repeating in my mind. *Follow your heart*. My heart was telling me I needed to be there for Jasper and his family.

"Well, my ship isn't for charter right now, so you can stay here, and you can charter it later."

The audacity of this man. "Your ship is always for sale; remember, you're a mercenary."

The look on Jasper's face made me want to take it back. I reached out to him, but he pushed my hand away as he walked to the front door as Marci was bringing the bags.

"You don't need to worry, Marci. The *princess* isn't going." Jasper spit out my title as though it left a bad taste in his mouth.

Marci looked at me without responding. "Please put all the bags in the transport." I got back into the transport.

CHAPTER 11

How dare she assume she's going to come with me? I can't worry about her and worry about Jasmine and the girls. Does she not understand how dangerous this could turn out to be?

I got back into the transport to travel to the spaceport. I would continue the conversation in the transport, as I wanted to get into the air as soon as possible. "Tahva, I can't let you go with me."

"Jasper, as I said before, you need me on the ship. I will grease palms if I must. The priority is to get Jasmine safe and to make those who took her pay."

"My ship isn't pretty; it isn't worthy royalty." I meant what I said. She was beautiful and deserved so much more than my ship. I love my ship, and I fully intend to die on it, but to think of Tahva travelling in it made me think about how inadequate it truly was.

"Do you think I'm only about being pretty or fancy?"

Honestly, I did think Tahva was primarily focused on being pretty and having all the attention. She has the nice transport, clothes, and everything she could ever want.

"Look at you; You have everything you desire at your fingertips."

"Oh, really? I have everything? I don't have my mother. Right now, I don't even have my father. My entire family is gone, and while I hope I can see my father again at some point, I know I won't see my mother again. She's gone, and I can't go fly and get her. You may not be able to bring your parents back, but you can get your sister, and I want to help."

I wasn't expecting the amount of emotion I got from Tahva. She'd told me about her father and the circumstances of why he left, but she hadn't said anything about her mother. There was a part of me that wanted Tahva by my side. She was incredible, but I also didn't want her to get hurt.

"But if you come with me, and I'm not saying you can, but if you do, what will happen here on Io with you gone? You can't just leave, right?" I honestly didn't know if she could or not. I was out of my element when it came to royalty and their responsibilities.

"I've already had Marci draft up a letter I'll send to the regency council once we're in the air. They can handle things for the time we are off moon. Since I haven't technically been appointed as queen, I can leave whenever I want. I don't require the fanfare kings and queens do when they leave."

"You thought about everything didn't you?" I was impressed by her desire to help me, someone she met recently. Sure, we were matched to marry, but it doesn't mean anything. We're two completely different people from, not only two different backgrounds, but two different parts of the solar system.

"Yes, I even already told Markus I'd be on the ship. He was surprised and may have asked if you'd approved it already. Which, of course, I told him you did." Tahva sat back with a smug smile.

"You did, did you? What did he say?" I folded my arms across my chest.

"He said there was no way you'd approved it, but he wasn't going to question it if I showed up with you."

I laughed out loud. I could imagine the face Markus made when Tahva told him she was going to be on the ship.

"I don't like it, but I'm not going to continue to argue with you because I have a feeling I would lose no matter what."

Before Tahva could say another word, we pulled into the spaceport. True to her word, the Stellar Kiwi was already on the runway. I could see Tak waiting for us, which meant Markus was ready to take-off. I had a crew who would follow me anywhere, including to our deaths, but their willingness to listen to Tahva and get everything ready was surprising. I realized without Tahva and Marci, I don't think my mind would've been able to focus enough to get everything ready.

When we stopped, I opened the door and held it open for Tahva. She said something to the driver and turned to me.

"I'm going to speak to the manager, but we should be cleared to take-off within 10 minutes if you think you can be ready by then."

Tak nodded.

"Yes, we can be ready whenever the manager says we're good to go. Tak, can you please grab the bags from the transport. I need to speak to Markus."

Tahva took off to the main building while Tak moved to grab the bags.

When I knew Tahva was far enough away she couldn't hear me speaking, I stopped Tak as he carried the bags onto the ship. "Tak, I need you to do something for me."

"Whatever you need, Boss."

"I need you to, no matter what, protect Tahva. Your number one priority is to protect her, even if it comes to choosing me or her. Do you understand?"

"But —" Tak protested.

"No Tak, I need you to protect her, and when we find Jasmine, to protect them both with your life. Promise me you'll protect them."

Tak looked like he was going to argue, but finally his shoulders slumped. "Yes, Boss. I promise I'll protect them. On my life."

"Thank you, Tak, I will not forget it, trust me."

He didn't say anything else as he took the bags onto the ship. I knew he didn't like what I'd asked him to do, but I also knew he would do it without question or hesitation.

***

I pretended not to be able to hear what Jasper told Tak, but Ioian hearing was good. I smiled knowing Jasper cared enough to protect me. He didn't need to worry; I could take care of myself if need be.

Walking into the main building, the spaceport's manager rushed over to me.

"Your Highness, the ship has been refueled as you requested, and I also had Markus, I think his name was, take the basket you asked for on board. Is there anything else you need from us?"

Reaching for him, I held his hand for a minute. "No Tika, you have been good to my family, and I know you did everything I asked. Please tell your family hello for me, and I've had Marci deliver something special to your spouse. I will see you again."

Tika dropped my hand and pulled me in for a hug. "Be safe, and if asked, I don't know anything about anything."

I hugged him back before releasing him and heading back to the Stellar Kiwi. No one, not even the regency council knew about Tika, or the fact he knew my father the way he did. Tika and my father had grown up together. Even though their individual paths had gone different directions, they'd stayed close, and I considered Tika an uncle. Right now, he was one of the only Ioians I could trust on the moon.

I smiled when I realized I did trust Jasper and his crew. Even though I had just met them, it felt like I had known them for a long time. While I was nervous to travel through space, I felt safe knowing Jasper was by my side.

"Everything good, Princess?" A large Titan was standing near the loading gate waiting for me.

"Yes, Tak, is it? Everything is good to go, and we can leave as soon as we want."

"Yes. It is Tak, and it will be my pleasure to show you to your seat. We aren't the most glamorous of ships, but she is one of the fastest."

"With what I have been told about the Stellar Kiwi, I would hope she's fast, or else I would be disappointed in the solar police."

Tak laughed as he showed me to a small cabin with a small bed on one side. The bag Marci had packed for me was sitting at the foot of the bed. On the other side of the room was a small desk with a chair. The basket I'd asked Tika to deliver was sitting on the desk.

"Your majesty, this is your room. I can show you more if this one isn't sufficient, or we can wait until we're in space."

"Tak, I'll stay here and get settled. You can let Jasper know where I am, but please don't worry about me. There's nowhere for me to go, and I'm sure you have other things you need to do than babysit me while we're travelling."

"I'll let them know, and I do have some things I need to accomplish before we get to Earth."

"Then get to it. I'll be here."

"I'll have Jasper check on you when his duties have been completed."

Tak left and I heard the door close softly. I sat in the chair looking at the basket. I hoped I wouldn't need to open it, but depending on what we find, I may have to.

The stress of the day, of the last month, finally caught up with me, and I decided to lay down on the bed and wait for take-off. Before I knew it, I was sound asleep.

***

"Markus, Tahva said she spoke to the port manager, and we're good to go the minute she gets back. Are we ready here?"

"Yes, we're good to go. We're all fueled up and waiting for the loading dock to close."

"Did we need to refuel?" I thought we'd had enough fuel to get us back to Earth without needing to pay the prices these outlying spaceports charged.

"Not really, but when the port manager says it's on the house, who am I to complain?"

Tahva must have arranged it. I'm going to have to repay her.

"I agree. I'm glad I don't have to worry about that." Looking at my intercell, I willed it to ring with Jasmine letting me know it was all a mistake. I knew in my heart it wouldn't happen, but I badly wanted it to.

"Boss, we'll find her. You know we will, right?"

"Will we, Markus? We don't know who took her or why. We don't know anything right now other than someone took her."

"Yes, I already have every single contact we have on it. I took some coin out of the reserve, but I knew you'd be fine with it. I've paid the ones who needed it, which were only a couple because most of them told me they were doing it for you."

Not all our contacts were on the good side of the law, and so it surprised me more didn't ask for payment. I would have paid them, even if it meant completely depleting our reserves to find Jasmine faster.

"It seems between you and Tahva, you have everything handled. Is there anything you need me to do?" I still felt in the same haze I was in when Cynthia had called me.

"Yes, you need to go rest. With everything on our side, we should be back to Earth in three days."

"Three days? It's usually a week-long trip."

There's no way Markus could make the trip in three days. We'd be picked up and arrested by the solar police before we could even hit Mars.

"It pays to have royalty on board. She had me call a branch of the solar police stationed near the asteroid belt, and we have clearance to travel as fast as we need. They even cleared a path through the belt for us."

I knew she was a princess, but to do all this for someone she didn't even know floored me.

"I guess you'd better get us there in three days." I patted his shoulder before turning to go to my cabin. While I didn't need sleep, I wanted to call Cynthia to make sure the girls were okay, let her know we'd be there in three days instead of a week, and we'd have a member of the royal family with us.

As I walked to my cabin, I saw Tak working in the armory alone. I was upset he wasn't with Tahva, since I'd given him strict instructions. "Where's the princess? I thought you were supposed to be watching her?"

"Don't worry. I took her to her cabin, and I locked the door from the outside before I left. It isn't like she's going to jump from the ship."

I felt my shoulders lower, and I let out the breath I didn't realize I was holding.

"You're right Tak, I'm sorry I was upset. I'm tense with everything going on, and I didn't mean to take it out on you. I trust you know what you're doing. Please continue working. If you need anything, I'll be in my cabin."

"You got it." Tak turned back to the armory to continue the tasks he was working on.

I had to walk past the cabin Tak had put Tahva in to get to my own. Since the Stellar Kiwi was so small, we each had a cabin, and we had two extras for when we had clients we were transporting. Since we usually moved materials, I don't remember the last time those cabins had been used. I hope Markus or Tak had freshened up the unused cabins before we'd arrived. I'm sure they did. They were more thoughtful about those sorts of things than I was.

I stopped at Tahva's cabin and knocked softly. I didn't hear anything, so I gently opened the door to make sure she was okay. Tahva was curled up on the bed, sound asleep. I reached into the closet, took out a blanket I knew we kept there, and put it over her. The ship usually stayed at a reasonable temperature, but with the speed we were going, I knew it would be colder than it had been on

Io. I whispered 'thank you' to her before turning out the light and closing the door.

She may be a spoiled princess, but I was starting to have real feelings for her. I couldn't focus on those while Jasmine was missing. Shaking my head, I entered my cabin. I knew Markus had everything right, so I laid down to take a nap myself.

CHAPTER 12

Waking up, I didn't remember where I was. The room was dark, but the blanket over me didn't feel like mine at home. I called out for Marci to turn on the lights, but no one answered. I closed my eyes again and thought about what was going on. *Yes, you're on a spaceship.* Once I remembered, I tried to find the light switch. I hit my shin on the chair before I fumbled to the door. I pressed it after I finally felt it to the right of the door. The room illuminated, and I closed my eyes to give them time to adjust to the brightness.

The last two weeks came back in a flash. From my father's attack, to him leaving, to meeting Jasper, everything.

Less than a month ago, I was a party girl with no responsibilities and no real cares on the moon other than what I was planning to wear to the next night at the club.

Now I'm poised to become Queen of Io. I'm to marry a Human, and I'm in a spaceship on my way to Earth in hopes of saving said Human's sister from whomever has kidnapped her.

I'm sure Roald would find all this amusing since he's been with us since I was young.

Was I doing the right thing? Leaving my moon, leaving my people, putting my life in the hands of someone I had known for such a small amount of time?

Every time I thought about Jasper, I felt warm, like I knew he would protect me, no matter what. I don't know why I felt this way, but I knew if someone tried to hurt me, he would be there. Growing up, I always felt protected but never in the way I did by Jasper.

With everything going on, I realized I hadn't eaten in who knows how many hours. I was so hungry. Hopefully they had a kitchen or something for food on board. My dad would tell me stories about how horrible the food was on some spaceships, and I hoped I wouldn't have to eat anything gross.

I went to the door to open it and found it locked.

They locked me in?

I panicked, thinking something had happened, and I was on the spaceship by myself. I was locked in, and no one was going to find me. I pounded on the door for what felt like forever until I finally heard the click.

"I see you're awake. Did you sleep well?" Tak was on the other side of the door holding a cup of something he handed me.

"What is this, and why did you lock me in my room?" I took the cup he offered me.

"It's Ioian tea. I figured you would want a piece of home even though we're far away from it. I locked you in your room because I didn't know if you walk in your sleep, and I didn't want you to be wandering around the ship without someone there.

I took a sip of tea. It reminded me of my mother, who would make me tea before bed.

"Thank you, this is good. I don't walk in my sleep, but I appreciate the thought. Trust me though, I won't wander anywhere without anyone. This is my first time on a spaceship."

"You, the princess, have never been off the moon? I can't believe it." Tak looked surprised.

"I haven't even been in the air. I'm not scared to fly, but I've never felt the need to. I had everything I needed on the moon, why go into space?"

"I guess you have a point. I've always wanted to be in space ever since I was a kid. Here, come with me, we'll get some food." Tak walked down the corridor as I followed, attempting to make conversation along the way.

"You're a Titanian right? How did you get with Jasper and Markus?"

Before Tak answered, he opened the door to the kitchen. There was a table with chairs, an icebox, a stove of sorts, and several cabinets with locks on their doors.

"It's like a mini kitchen. Do you cook?"

"Yes, ma'am. We cook and eat a meal a day together, and the other two meals are on your own. We have ready-made meals, but you can also cook if you want. Is there something specific you want?"

"I know this may be asking a lot, but could you make me waffles?" I didn't know if they had a waffle iron, but it didn't hurt to ask.

"I can make you waffles. How many would you like?" Tak got out the ingredients. I sat there and watched.

"Start making them, and I'll tell you when to stop."

"A woman after my own heart. Your wish is my command. I probably should make some for the Captain and Markus too. They love my waffles."

"You never answered my questions." I sat back in the chair sipping on the tea.

"I'm Titanian. To answer your other question, it's complicated, but we have time. I met Jasper and Markus over ten years go."

I was getting done with a day of work and was heading to the store to get food for dinner before going home. To get there, I had to go through the spaceport on Titan. I didn't have a vehicle, so I walked everywhere. At the time, I still lived with my mom and two younger brothers. My dad had died in a mining accident when they were initially creating one of the new towns. I supported my mom and family by working as a machinist for a local repair shop repairing spaceships. It was the closest to space I ever thought I would get, and I was going to soak up everything I could from my bosses and the ships I worked on. I was thinking about the new ship coming in that I would get to work on after dinner. It was a newer model from Earth.

As I was walking through the spaceport, I saw a car pull up to a ship taxiing near the main building. I thought it was odd because the port manager didn't usually let vehicles close to a moving ship. I continued walking but I watched the car. As I approached the end of the spaceport, I heard what I thought were fireworks, but they were coming from behind me where the car was. I looked back and saw two men standing near the spaceship with guns drawn. I realized what I thought were fireworks was gunfire, and I had to get out of there. I turned and ran into a piece of metal hanging off a building. The noise attracted the attention of the two men near the ship. I didn't want to go home because if they thought I had seen something, which I hadn't, it would've put my mom and brothers in danger. So instead, I went back to the repair shop.

As I ran into the shop, I literally ran into Markus. He grabbed me by the arms, making sure I didn't fall over. He asked what was wrong, and I didn't want to tell him. If I did and he was part of whatever was going on, I would be putting myself in even more danger. I was paranoid. I told him nothing was wrong, and I wanted to make sure I started working on the ship as soon as I could. I knew he didn't believe me, but he also didn't ask any more questions. He told me what needed to be done and showed me to the ship.

I couldn't believe I was working on this ship. Everyone knew about the Stellar Kiwi, but this was the first time it was in our shop. The things they needed weren't important, and it took me only a couple of hours to finish. I went to find Markus and found him and Jasper in the lounge, talking. Markus asked me to sit down. Jasper told me he was impressed with how quickly I repaired the issues. He also asked why I was in such a hurry earlier. I tried to tell the same lie I'd told Markus, but Jasper looked at me like he could read my thoughts. Since the two men at the port were Titanians, and Jasper and Markus were Human, I had to take a chance they weren't involved.

Jasper and Markus listened to what I had to say. When I was done, they looked at each other, and Markus got up and left. I had no idea what was going on, but Jasper started talking about how they were a relatively new crew, and they needed someone who could repair their ship while in space because it took time to land and find a repair shop. If some of the easier things could be done in space, they wouldn't have to land as much. I told him I couldn't leave my mother and brothers because I was the sole provider. When he told me how much I could be making, and they would also send money back to Titan for my family, I knew it was all my dreams come true. I would be in space, but my family would still be provided for. Jasper told me to think about it, but I knew it was the answer to everything. I said yes immediately, and Jasper told me Markus would go home with me to get my stuff and let my family know what was going on. Markus and Jasper made sure to tell me to not let my family know what the ship was called because if those two men did somehow figure out who I was, my family wouldn't be able to tell them anything. I did exactly that, and I have been with Jasper and Markus ever since.

"Have you seen your family since you left?" The more I found out about Jasper, the more I realized he was a good guy.

"Yes, every time we stop on Titan for any amount of time, I make sure to visit my mom. My brothers are now grown and have families of their own, but I get to see them at least once a year. I tried to get my mother to move to Earth and live near Markus' mother and Jasmine, but she wanted to stay on Titan."

"Did those men ever find out about you? What happened? If I'm being too nosy, please don't feel like you have to answer."

Before Tak answered, he brought over a large plate of waffles. As I lifted the first forkful to my mouth, I heard Markus and Jasper walking toward the kitchen.

"Are those waffles I smell?" Jasper asked as he and Markus made themselves a cup of coffee before sitting down.

"You know they are."

"Perfect, I hope you cooked them the way I like them."

"To answer your question, from what we were able to gather after leaving was an unknown number of individuals had attacked a ship carrying funds to help the Titanian government. No one ever figured out how the attackers knew about the ship, and the money was never recovered."

The way Tak looked at Jasper and Markus made me wonder if they maybe knew more about it than they were letting on, but I wasn't going to ask them.

Instead, I ate the waffles. I don't know what I expected, but they were delicious. I could get used to Tak's cooking.

"How do you feel about being on my spaceship?"

"So far, so good. I got some sleep, I'm eating some great food, and I'm surrounded by good company."

"Wait until we get to Earth, and you get to meet Cynthia and the girls."

Jasper's comment stopped me mid bite. "Wait, I'm not ready to meet people. I didn't bring clothes for meeting people."

All three of them laughed at my comment.

Markus was the first to speak. "My mother could care less what you're wearing. She'll be so happy to meet royalty. As for the two girls, a real-life princess? They'll think you're the absolute best. In fact, you may outrank both their Uncle Jasper and me. Maybe it would be best if you didn't meet them after all."

I laughed. "Now I definitely have to meet them."

***

The next two days were filled with Markus and I speaking to our contacts trying to get a lead on where Jasmine had been taken. We had some solid leads but needed to get to Earth first and get Cynthia and the girls. I didn't want them still on Earth when we found Jasmine because whoever took her could go after them next, which we couldn't allow to happen.

I also spent as much time with Tahva as I could. The more I spoke to her and got to know her, the more I realized she was actually a good person. Much better than the persona she gave off. From the things she'd done to help me find Jasmine, to being there to listen when I spoke, I felt like we were growing together. It was strange going from complete strangers to whatever we were now in such a short amount of time.

"Boss, we're about enter Earth's orbit," Markus announced over the intercom system.

I paused the card game Tahva and I were playing in the kitchen.

"Do you want to see Earth from the bridge?"

"Are you sure? I don't want to be in the way."

"Absolutely, we need to go soon so you can see Earth from space. It's a beautiful sight."

"Let's go."

I held Tahva's hand as we walked toward the bridge. When the door opened, all the window panels were open, and you could see Earth getting closer. I heard a small gasp from Tahva.

"It's so beautiful."

I looked at Tahva, and all I could see was the wonder in her eyes.

She smiled, which caused me to smile.

"Yes, it is, and so are you." I kissed her cheek before directing her to her seat next to the captain's chair. I didn't tend to use these chairs often, instead preferring to stand near Markus.

"We should be on the ground in 10. Please prepare the ship for landing," Markus announced.

I showed Tahva how to buckle in. Sometimes the landing was rough depending on the cross winds.

Turning to Markus, I asked, "You called your mom to let her know where to meet us, right?"

"Before we got close to orbit. She'll be at our designated location within 5 of us landing."

"Sounds good, and did you hear anything from your contact yet?"

"No, I haven't, but I should be soon if their intel was correct."

"Keep me appraised."

I looked at Tahva. "I want you to stay on the ship. Tak and I'll get out and make sure everything is good, then Cynthia and the girls will board the ship. Do you understand?"

"Are you sure I can't get out? I want to put my feet on Earth."

"Not this time, please. I promise you I will bring you back to Earth in the future, but please for my sanity, this time, stay on the ship."

"I will."

The minute we landed, I was up and running to the back. I heard Markus tell Tahva to stay on the bridge because they could see all sides of the ship from there. Tak handed me a weapon, and we ran to the loading dock. I didn't expect any trouble, but if they'd kidnapped Jasmine to get to me, they knew I would come back to Earth, and I wasn't going to let anything happen to my ship or those I swore to protect.

Tak jumped down before the loading dock was on the ground. He looked both ways and motioned it was safe.

I left the ship and went to the nearest building. Knocking three times, I waited for the door to open.

Cynthia was standing there with a pipe in her hand. Seeing it was me, she dropped the pipe and hugged me.

I motioned for Tak to maintain watch while Cynthia moved to pick up the bags. I grabbed three while she called for the girls and grabbed the fourth. Two little redheads popped up from behind a bale of hay. When they saw it was me, they rushed me and hugged my legs.

"We don't have a lot of time, is this everything?"

"Yes, those are all the bags, but the girls have Chloe and Chad."

"Why do the girls have them?"

"I had Jasmine's partner come and pick up the rest of the animals, but you know how the girls are with these two. I think it'll make Jasmine happy to see them as well. They're the first breeding pair she had."

I couldn't argue with Cynthia's logic, so I told the girls to grab them and go. Jannie had little collars on them and was carrying them. Juju held on to Jannie's shirt as they walked.

Seeing nothing of concern, I called Tak over to help with the stuff. He picked up the giggling girls and carried them onto the ship.

When they were on the ship, I turned to Cynthia.

"How are they holding up?"

"Jannie is trying to be brave for Juju, and Juju doesn't understand what's going on. We're going to get her back, right?"

"One way or another, Jasmine will be back on my ship. So you know, we have a guest on the ship."

"Oh?" I swore Cynthia's eyes twinkled.

"I'm assuming Markus already told you?"

"Markus could never keep a secret from me."

I shook my head as I picked up the bags and carried them to the ship. The minute I got on the ship, the loading door started to close.

"It's going to be a tight fit, so you can have my quarters."

"I'm not going to take your cabin. We'll figure something out." Leave it to Cynthia not to worry about her own comfort.

***

107

"Princess, you can let go of my hand now. I think you broke my fingers." Markus was looking at his hand shaking it.

"I did not but thank you. They're on the ship now, right? We can take-off?"

"Yes and yes, do you want to go meet them?"

Suddenly, I was nervous to meet Markus' mother and Jasper's two nieces. I'd heard a lot about them over the last three days, and I knew how much Markus and Jasper loved them. *What if they don't like me? What if they think I'm strange, and the girls are scared of me?*

"We should let them get settled in, and I can meet them after. I don't want to rush anything."

"Don't be nervous. They'll love you like Jasper does." Markus realized what he had said, and his face turned red. "Please don't tell him what I said. I want to keep my fingers, even if they're already broken."

Wait, Jasper loves me? Did I hear right? I didn't say anything, but my mind was racing. Did I love Jasper? Did I even know Jasper? He was a good man, at least when it came to those he cared about. He was essentially a pirate, though. Well, a captain to the highest bidder, anyway. I never strayed from the law. It was relatively easy to do since Io didn't have many laws to start with. Heck, I never even drove past the speed limit. I barely drove as it was as most vehicles were self-driven, but once in a while I enjoyed using the manual option. I didn't even do any of the club drugs and always maintained sobriety when I was at a club. I knew other people didn't, but I hated not being in control of myself. The music was enough to sooth and help me, so I didn't need more. How would it look for a princess to be married to a pirate? Would he still want to work and captain the ship once we got married? Would I want him around all the time? So many questions, not enough answers, and right now, time was running out on all of us it seemed.

As I thought about it, I watched Jasper and Tak leave the ship again.

"Why are they leaving again?"

"Jasper is likely checking on something."

"Why didn't do he do that the first time?" Jasper walked to the door of a nearby building. I was nervous and wanted them all back on the ship.

"Your Highness, please sit down and take a deep breath. This isn't the first time Jasper has had to leave the ship with weapons, and Tak is very good at his job."

"I can't relax. What if whoever took Jasmine wanted us to do exactly what we're doing? They wanted us to come get the girls and they would come back and attack us."

"If they do, we'll be ready for them. In the meantime, sit down and relax. They'll be back in no time. You can watch from the window to make sure everything is okay."

Suddenly, the door to the building opened and Jasper called over to Tak. As Tak walked over, two young red-headed girls ran out and jumped on him.

These must be Jasper's nieces.

Jasper walked out with an older blonde woman who walked with her back straight and tall. In her arms was a bag. I looked over at Markus, and he was smiling. I could see the family resemblance. I watched until Jasper and Cynthia walked onto the ship and stood to greet the three. I knew it wasn't my ship, but being a princess and having been taught to be the hostess was hard to turn off.

I walked back toward the cabins and heard Jasper and Cynthia arguing about where she was going to be staying. Jasper wanted her to take the captain's cabin, but she said she wouldn't take it from him. Before I realized what I was doing, I was speaking.

"May I interrupt?" My comment caused Cynthia and Jasper to stop arguing and look at me.

"Cynthia, may I present you with Princess Tahva of Io."

Cynthia bowed. "I wish I could say it was a pleasure to meet you, but things aren't the best right now."

"I completely understand, and I appreciate your honesty. If I'm not imposing too much, I would like to offer you my cabin. The girls can stay in the other cabin."

"Princess, I cannot possibly take your cabin. I can stay in one with the girls." Cynthia was going to argue with me.

"No, there's only one bed, and there's not enough space for you and the girls in one small bed. Please take mine. I'm not a wilting flower. I'll figure something out."

Jasper looked at me, questioning.

"Thank you, and I'll take you up on your offer."

"Great, let me show you my cabin, and I'll grab my stuff."

"I'll take the girls from Tak and show them their cabin. I'm sure they're tired and ready for a nap."

I turned away from Jasper and Cynthia, knowing she would follow me to the cabin. I opened the door and walked inside. The room was big enough for two people to stand comfortably, so while Cynthia stood there, I put everything into my bag. I grabbed it and the basket. I turned to leave when Cynthia stopped me.

"Thank you again. I know how much you've done to help get Jasper to us and to help rescue Jasmine. Please be careful with Jasper."

"Why should I be careful?"

"After losing his parents, Jasmine and the girls are his entire family. He loves deeply and loyally. If you plan on being with him, plan on being with him forever, because once you start down the path, there is no going back."

I was a little taken aback. "Thank you for your concern. I am much the same way as he is, although my family is much smaller than his, with only my father. I don't know if our relationship will become more than what we are now, but I already treasure him as a friend."

"I'm glad. He's a good man, regardless of what he and my son do for a living."

I nodded and walked out to the hall. I could hear giggling coming from down the hall and as I approached the door, I saw two girls jumping on a bed with Jasper watching them, smiling. I put my bag and basket down and stepped into the room.

"Girls, stop. I want you to meet someone."

Both girls stopped jumping and looked up at Jasper when they realized I was standing there. The taller of the two's eyes widened. I wasn't used to kids, only spending time with them when I had no other choice. For some reason, their earlier giggling had drawn me in. Even with what was going on, they were still happy, and their happiness made me smile.

"Jannie and Juju, please say hello to Princess Tahva."

Jannie was the first one to speak. "Are you a real princess?"

Juju stood there looking between her sister and me.

"Yes, I am the princess on my moon. My father is the king."

Jannie looked sad for a second. "My father is dead."

I didn't know what to say, so I looked at Jasper for help.

Jasper picked up Jannie and Juju and hugged them. "Their father was on the ship I told you about that had been attacked, and he was killed a few years ago."

Still not knowing what to say, I stood there for a second. "I'm sorry, my mom is dead."

Jannie looked at me for a second before she tried to reach out from Jasper's arms to mine. I didn't want to be rude, which was weird because this is a child, but I felt a connection to her. I reached for her, and she hugged me around the neck. It was as if she understood what I was feeling. I felt my eyes start to mist up, so I hugged her back. It was like she understood how I felt without saying anything. How did someone in such a little body have so much empathy and wisdom? I heard what sounded like a combination of a hiss and a spit. Looking about, I saw two little brown heads peeking out from behind Juju. I dropped Jannie onto the bed and jumped back into Jasper's arms.

"What… What are those?"

Juju and Jannie laughed as each grabbed one of the small, brown creatures.

Jasper was the first to stop laughing and answered, "These are quokkas, Chloe and Chad."

I'd never had pets growing up, so for me to see these girls holding these creatures and these creatures in turn snuggling their noses into the girl's necks caused a pain of regret. My mother and father didn't like animals as they said it would cause more work for the housekeepers.

"What are quokkas?"

"Quokkas are small animals from Earth. They were almost wiped out back in the 21st century, but biologists and farmers started a breeding program. My sister is one of the top quokka breeders on

Earth. She's almost single handedly repopulated New Zealand and Australia, their natural territory. Her project was wrapping up. When she was kidnapped, Cynthia had Jasmine's partner come get the remaining quokkas from the property, but Chloe and Chad are part of the family."

I hesitantly approached the one Jannie was holding. I carefully reached out, hoping it would smell and not bite.

"It's okay. You can pet her. She loves pets, especially near her ears."

Jannie's prompting had me touching this little ball of fur. When I got closer to it, I realized they weren't solid brown as I had thought but different shades of brown with white fur as well. I touched its ears, and noticed they were fuzzy and soft. Its little, darker nose wiggled. As I was petting Chloe, I realized we may not have food for them. In fact, I didn't even know what they ate.

"Jasmine started the project with these two, and they have become pets to the girls. Jasmine received permission to keep them once the project was over. We didn't think it would end this way."

"I'm glad they got to stay since they look happy. What do they even eat?"

"Yeah, they're really attached to the girls. Even more so than to Jasmine, and she's the one who takes care of them. To answer your question, they're herbivores, so they eat grass, plants, fruit, and veggies, so don't worry. No matter where they live, there will be food for them."

I was glad to hear they'd be okay. It was one thing for them to be taken from their home, but to not have anything to eat would be horrible. With nothing else to say, I stood there thinking about this group of people and animals now on this ship. Thankfully, Jasper stepped in.

"Enough laughing and goofing off. Girls, please take a nap?"

"Uncle Jasper, where are we going?"

I saw Jasper look over at me before answering. "I think we're going to go to Io and drop off you, Juju, Tahva, and Cynthia."

I started to argue, but his look stopped me.

"Before you go find Momma?"

"Yup, before Uncle Markus and I go and get your mom."

"Momma needs help." Jannie's eyes were half opened when she answered. Juju was already snuggled under the covers.

"Go to sleep, girls. We'll be here when you wake up." Before he had finished talking, the girls were fast asleep, Jannie holding her sister.

I quietly walked out the door and went to pick up my bag and basket.

Jasper got there first and picked up both. "I got these, so I'll give you my cabin, and I can stay on the bridge."

"Absolutely not. If I'm going to be in your cabin, you will be as well. I'm not making you sleep in a chair." I was adamant he was not going to sleep sitting up. He was the captain, after all.

CHAPTER 13

Did she say what I think she said?

"You want to share a room with me?" I didn't want to look shocked, but it was less than a week ago when we were fighting over her even coming with us. Now she wants to share a room?

"I figure I can sleep while you're on the bridge, or vice versa. As long as I have a place for my bag and the basket Marci made for me, I'm good. Remember Io is on a different schedule, so I can stay up for a lot longer than Humans normally can."

My chest fell a little. For some reason, I wanted her to want me in bed with her. I was getting ahead of myself, and I needed to rein myself back in. She was being considerate, not wanting me to be with her.

"I've trained myself as well to stay up in the event we needed to do something. I think we can arrange different sleep schedules." I swore I saw her look a little sad, but I couldn't tell for sure, and I wasn't going to ask her

"This arrangement will work." She was back to being chilly.

I walked to the cabin thinking about what this meant for us, and for our future, if we even had one. There's a saying about how trauma can bring people together, but I don't want us being together because of shared concern or a need for something or someone. I opened the door and put her bag on the bed. My cabin was somewhat bigger than the guest cabins, with a queen size bed versus a smaller twin-size. My desk was also larger and had drawers. The guest desks didn't have drawers. I also had a bathroom attached directly to my cabin, while the guest cabins all shared one. Markus and Tak's cabins were similar to mine, but with smaller beds since they weren't as tall as me. They shared a bathroom, versus having their own.

When I was considering starting this company, I went to Markus and asked him to join me. He participated in the process of the ship build as much, if not more, than I did. Knowing we didn't plan on having a lot of transports, we opted for fewer, smaller cabins and more cargo space. We also opted for a larger walk-in armory and a larger mechanic area. Those were decisions we agreed on because we didn't know what the future would bring in terms of needing repairs or weaponry. We went bigger than needed in hopes of not needing to renovate the ship in the future. Unless we decided on getting a new, larger one altogether. The addition of Tak was perfect because we didn't have to stop as often for repairs. He was also a good marksman, which we haven't needed much, but it was nice having his skills on board.

"Do you need anything?" If she wanted to be professional and cold, I could be professional and cold. I'd also be dropping her off on Io. I'm not going to go searching for my sister with her kids on board, especially since it could get dangerous. If I lose anyone... I don't want to lose everyone. The fear of loss had been on my mind since I met Tahva. My job is dangerous, or it can be. The dangerous ones usually paid the most, but with the possibility of marrying Tahva, I'm worried about leaving her alone if something were to happen to me, like with Raf and Jasmine. The pain she must go through on a daily basis. I was so deep in thought I almost didn't hear Tahva respond to me.

"No, but I think I'll help Tak with dinner."

"Really? Yeah, I'm sure he'd appreciate the help." I finally realized I was still holding the basket. Putting it on the desk, I couldn't tell what was in it. "What's in the basket?"

"Just some stuff from home I may need."

Well, that's cryptic, but I'm sure it's makeup or something.

"I'm going to get back to the bridge to see if Markus needs a break or if he's found out anything about Jasmine. You know your way around the ship now. Please consider it your home, at least until we get back to Io." I started to walk out, but Tahva stopped me.

"Actually, I wanted to talk to you about that. I'm not going to stay on Io, I'm going to come with you."

"Tahva, we've talked about this already. You need to stay on the moon. Io is your home; you need to stay here. I need to ask you something as well."

"Yeah, what do you need?"

"While you're staying on the moon, I need Cynthia and the girls to stay with you while we head back out to search for Jasmine."

"They can obviously stay at the mansion, but I won't be staying with them. I told you. I'm coming with you, and I'm not going to fight you over it."

"Listen, I have to go see if Markus needs help, but you and I will talk about this again later. Do you understand?"

"Yes Captain Jasper, we'll talk about this later, but rest assured, I will prevail."

I couldn't argue with her. I was caught between wanting to kiss her and wanting to throttle her. Instead of doing anything, I turned and walked out of the cabin. I could hear her sigh before the tapping of her shoes could be heard going toward the kitchen. Shaking my head, I walked down the hall to the bridge.

"Tahva already getting under your skin, Boss?"

"Haha very funny. Listen, and I don't want to repeat myself, but Tahva is to get off this ship on Io, and she is to stay with our family in the mansion. Do you understand?"

"Oh, I understand, but you're going to have to fight her, not me, Boss." Markus chuckled while standing to go to his cabin.

"You think after saying all that, you get to leave the bridge?"

"Absolutely. It's your turn to watch. Oh yeah, I'm supposed to be getting a message from one of our contacts regarding Jasmine. He thinks he may have a lead."

"Keep me updated. Go take a nap or get some food. Speaking food, Tahva is going to help Tak with dinner."

"Does Tak know?"

"Nope, and with her arguing about staying on Io, I figured I'd let her surprise Tak."

"You're cruel. You may have everyone else fooled, but not me, Boss, not me."

I slapped Markus' shoulder before he walked out. I couldn't run my business or my ship without him. I probably couldn't run my life without him either.

Sitting, I thought about everything from over the last two weeks. Meeting Tahva, starting to like her, Jasmine going missing, us travelling back to Earth. Everything and how it's affected me. I don't think my life will ever be the same. I don't know what to do with that information.

I heard Tak yelling and smiled to myself. He must have found out Tahva was in his kitchen. The next hour went by relatively smoothly. We were on our way back to Io and hopefully Markus' contact had information to lead us to Jasmine. I had to get her back, not only for the girls, but for myself. I'd already lost our mother and father. I couldn't lose her too.

***

I started going through the kitchen cabinets to see what I was working with. When I was younger, I used to be in the kitchen with my mother and the chef, and I would help them cook. I used to love it. I wonder when I stopped loving it. Probably around the same time she died. I pulled out some fruit and vegetables. I may not know Earth or Titan food, but you couldn't go wrong with basic food. I searched for a knife, and when I found one, I cut small pieces of each food off and tasted each one. I was tasting this round orange colored fruit when Tak came in.

"What are you doing in my kitchen?"

"Well first of all, I think it's Jasper's kitchen. I was going to help you cook."

"Oh, were you? Do you even know what you're holding?"

"I assume it's a fruit because it's sweet. It isn't Ioian or Tritonian since I haven't seen one before."

"It's called an orange. It is a fruit, from Earth."

"Wait, it's orange, and is called an orange? Humans aren't too creative, are they?"

Tak started pulling out pots and pans. "Not really at times, but they do have some good food."

"Let me help you. I used to love cooking, and I think I want to get back into it."

"Are you sure? Because I'll put you to work."

I rolled up my sleeves. "Yes, put me to work, chef."

Tak gave me vegetables to cut up while explaining what vegetables they were and what they could be used to cook. It was interesting learning about all these different kinds of foods. I think once everything was straightened out and we got Jasmine back, I would start cooking again. At least occasionally when my responsibilities as the queen didn't take precedence.

Within thirty minutes we had a stew Tak explained was popular on Earth. He felt an earthen dish would be good for Cynthia and the girls since they are most used to it. It was full of vegetables, and the rich broth was full of herbs. I hoped everyone would like it. We don't have this type of stew on Io, and it turned out delicious. I was proud of myself, even though Tak only let me cut vegetables and stir things. He even slapped my hand when I tried to add the one seasoning in the cabinets I knew.

Tak announced over the intercom system dinner was ready, and I went to tell Jasper myself. I walked toward the bridge, and the doors opened to Markus and Jasper talking.

"Guys, it's dinner time."

"Great, I'll get Mom and the girls." Markus left the room, leaving Jasper and I alone on the bridge.

"Were you and Markus talking about where Jasmine might be? Did we find her?"

"Markus has a lead he's going to follow up on after dinner, and if it's solid, we'll get you all to Io and head out."

Instead of arguing with him again about how I'm not going to stay on Io, I nodded and turned to go back to the kitchen. It would be a tight fit, but we'll make it work. Jasper and I were the last to enter and with how much food was on the table, I didn't think there would be any left for me.

"Jasper, Tahva, over here. I saved you some food from these piranhas over here."

Both girls giggled at Markus' calling them piranhas.

"They're more like Tasmanian devils," Jasper replied as he sat with me at the end of the table.

"Please excuse me, but what are these piranhas and Tasmanian devils you're talking about?" I assumed they were animals, but why are they calling kids an animal?

Jasper and Markus looked at each other before laughing. "Piranhas are earth-based fish who eat other animals. They go into a frenzy when food is around. Think of one piece of food and, like, 50 fish all rushing at it."

"I can see how people rushing Tak's food is like a bunch of piranhas. His food is tasty. But what about a ... what did you call them ... Tasmanian devils?"

Markus took this one while Jasper continued to eat. "Tasmanian devils are carnivores who are little bundles of energy. They're marsupials who have little pockets on their front side they raise their babies in. Think of quokkas but darker colored and fierce. Screaming and powerful, they will cause a mess and growl about it."

"Like the girls when they're ramped up and having fun, not in a negative way."

"Yup, exactly. It's common on Earth to compare actions or personality types with something relatable. So, the Tasmanian devil is an animal from our region."

"I'm starting to understand some of your Human ways."

Tak spoke up for the first time, "We do something similar on Titan. My mom used to call me her petit chou chou. She said it was a vegetable from Earth."

Cynthia almost snorted her food out of her nose. "It is a vegetable. It's actually a cabbage."

"Wait, my mom was calling me a cabbage?"

Cynthia laughed again. "Yes, it's a French saying. My mom was French and used to call me it as well growing up. It's a term of endearment you call someone you love."

"That's sweet. I didn't know; I figured it was something she called me. But still, a vegetable?"

The whole group laughed at Tak trying to figure out why his mom called him a vegetable.

***

While we were eating, I couldn't keep from looking at Tahva. Her laughter and questions made me smile. I know we'd been through a lot but seeing her still smile made it all the worthwhile. Now, if we can find Jasmine safe and sound.

After dinner, Marcus followed me back to the bridge. Tahva had stayed to help Tak clean up, and Cynthia and the girls went back to the girl's cabin to get cleaned up before they watched a movie.

The space comm alerted to a message and Markus checked it. He read it over, got on the space comm, and spoke to someone. I could hear Jasmine's name, but I knew there wasn't a point in hovering over him to get information. He would get it all and let me know what he found out. Patience was never my strong suit, and it felt like Markus had been on the space comm for hours when he finally clicked off, put his headset down, and turned toward me.

"Well, what did your contact say?"

"Our contact has heard about Jasmine and where she was heading. It looks like she was picked up and was enroute to Triton."

"We must have crossed paths with them at some point after we left Io."

"Apparently, it's not like we knew, you know?"

"I know, but it's frustrating because we could've possibly have intercepted her."

Markus stared at me for a solid fifteen seconds before he answered.

"And what? Board a random ship with who knows what on it in the hopes your sister is on it? We aren't space police. It's not like we have any authorization to board another ship."

"Why do you always have to be the voice of reason?"

"Because if I wasn't, you wouldn't have one, and you would get in trouble or crash this beautiful ship."

"I swear, sometimes you care more about this ship than you do me."

"Obviously I care more about the ship. Without her, I wouldn't have any money."

"Haha. What's the plan?"

I knew what Markus was trying to do by saying what he had. He was trying to get my mind off what was going on. I admit, it worked for a minute.

"Our contact tracked her to the asteroid belt, and she was handed off to another ship. She's being held in a hangar at the Spaceport. Our contact as seen a lot of activity today, so he doesn't know how long they'll be there."

"What are you saying?"

"I'm saying as of right now, we don't have time to stop on Io. And we need Tahva, at least for right now, to help grease the palms of space police if we need her to."

"You're saying you want me to take Tahva, as well as your mom and my nieces, into what could possibly be a dangerous situation?"

"I don't want to, but my mom has some skills which may be useful if needed, and Tahva and my mom will protect the girls if needed. I think this is our best chance to get Jasmine before they move her, if they plan on moving her."

"I know you're right, but I don't like it."

"You don't have to like it."

"I know. I guess I'll go tell Tahva the good news." I begrudgingly walked out. I know she'd be happy about it, but I still didn't think it was a good idea.

"How is this good news?"

"She wanted to come with us, and I wanted her to stay on Io with Cynthia and the girls."

"Good news for her, but not for you. Why don't you admit your feelings to her?"

"Markus, I don't know what's going to happen between us. My priority is finding Jasmine and getting Tahva home, beyond that, I don't know."

"I understand, but sooner or later you need to let her know."

"You can keep reminding me while we rescue Jasmine and figure out who's behind all this."

I swear I saw him roll his eyes. "Will do."

 I found Tahva with Cynthia and the girls watching a movie.

"Where did you find popcorn?"

"Tak had it squirreled away from you, Jasper. Apparently, you and Markus will eat it all on the bridge and leave a mess," Cynthia responded while taking a handful of popcorn from the bowl.

"Ungrateful…" I started before Tahva looked up at me with a raised eyebrow. I remembered why I had come in.

"Hey Tahva, can I speak to you in the hall?"

Without responding, she got up and walked past me into the hall.

Once she was in the hall, she turned back toward me. "What do you need?"

"I wanted to give you an update on what's happening. We have confirmation Jasmine is on Triton."

"Does this mean you'll be stopping on Io in some vain attempt to get me to stay there?"

"Actually no. We don't have time to stop because if we do, we may risk them moving her before we can get there."

"Jasper, I know you don't think I'll be useful, but I will."

"I wanted to talk to you about that. I need you to get on the space comm with whoever you can and make it so we can get to Triton's spaceport without any interference."

"Please, I can do more."

I watched Tahva walk to the bridge. I had no idea what she meant, but I was going to leave her to it. I don't know why I was having such a hard time trusting or believing in her. I trusted Tak from the day he ran into the hangar, and Markus has had my back my entire life.

∗∗∗

Who the heck does he think he is, telling me what to do, and when to do it? If he thinks I'll jump at his beck and call? Absolutely not. He must be out of his damn mind.

I was still fuming as I stomped onto the bridge.

"What's got your goat?"

"What are you talking about? I don't have a goat. What's a goat?"

Markus laughed. "A goat is an Earth animal, and 'got your goat' is a figure of speech about being angry over something or at someone."

"Well, Jasper does. He thinks he knows everything.

"He usually does, but what is it this time?"

"He feels he's being benevolent by *allowing* me to accompany you to Triton, as long as I do something for him. I'm not some puppet who will do stuff at their master's orders." I was pacing, clenching and unclenching my hands. I was so upset.

Markus stood and put his hands on my shoulders, stopping me from pacing. "Slow down, Jasper may not be the best communicator, but I know two things about him. First, he doesn't expect you to do anything you don't want to do, and second, he tries his hardest to protect those he cares about. He doesn't want you to go so you and the girls can stay safe. We don't know what we are walking into. I know I'd prefer if you, mom, and the girls weren't there either, but it's a moot point right now since we have to get

126

there. Don't forget you offered to help with the space police and such. He's saying it's time for help now."

Taking a breath and realizing Markus was right, I shouldn't take it personally. I wonder why I'm so on edge right now. I usually have something snarky to reply with and then go about my day, but when Jasper says something, I get upset. There has never been another man who caused a reaction like this. I don't know what it means, but right now I can't think about it.

"You're right, let me rethink everything. What do we know?"

Markus ran down what we had learned about Jasmine being on Triton and where she was currently being held. Depending on how fast we could leave once I talked to the space police, it would take us about five days to get there. If they decided to move her, five days was a long time.

"My dad's friend on Triton is the port master, so I think he can at least get eyes on the hangar and make sure they don't get permission to leave. He controls the port pretty well."

"How long as he been there?"

"Only a short time. The old port master used to let a lot of things slide, and it's caused some issues. Why do you ask?"

"No reason, we were there not too long ago getting supplies to Europa, and it looked cleaner than before."

"Yeah, I remember him meeting with my father and letting him know his priority was cleaning everything up."

"I'm glad he did. We'll have the space police on our side, and the port with eyes on the hangar. We have three fighters on the ship, do you have anyone else?"

"Actually, we need to stop by Mars first, at least I think she's there." I was trying to formulate the best group.

"We're about 2 hours away from Mars. Who do you want to pick up?"

"Let me make a fast call, and I'll let you know if we need to stop."

Markus motioned toward the space comm as I dialed Marci.

"How are you holding up?"

"Good, we picked up Jasper's nieces and Markus' mother. We're heading to Triton. Can you get me Botha's contact information, and quickly?"

"Yeah, just a minute." Marci disappeared from the screen. Within a minute she was back on. "Here it is, but I know she isn't at home."

"How do you know?"

"Before she left, she said she was going to be going to Europa to check on some of the crew there and after, head to Triton because her sister or brother were living there. She wanted to visit them since she was on this side of the belt."

"That's the best news I've heard recently, Marci. Thank you. And Marci, be prepared for us in about 10 days?" I looked over at Markus who nodded.

"How many should I prepare for?"

Quickly counting how many, I told her, "Two girls who should be in the same room, five adults, and two quokkas."

"What's a quokka?"

"A small rodent looking animal." I could see by the face she was making she didn't know what to think.

"Do you want them to be in any specific room or do they need their own room?"

I never gave Marci enough credit. No matter how I'd treated her in the past or pushed stuff onto her, she did it. She could anticipate what I needed before I did, and between her and Roald, I'm sure they kept me in one piece, or at least appearing as one since my mother died.

Laughing at the thought of them being alone, Jasper replied, "They can be with the girls. Can you make sure the chef prepares some fruit and vegetables without seasoning or dressing for them?"

Shaking her head, Marci laughed. "I should take an image of the chef's face when I tell them they will be making food for rodents."

"Make sure you get an image for me, will you?"

"Be safe, and you got the basket, right?"

"I did, and you packed everything I requested?"

"And a couple extras."

"Thank you, Marci. You probably won't hear from me again until we get back into space from Triton."

"If I haven't heard from you in ten days, what do you want me to do?"

"I want you to call the port master in Triton. He'll have eyes on the situation, but don't call him unless you haven't heard from us. I don't want it to tie back to me if he's compromised."

"Is it bad?"

"Marci, I don't know, it looks that way, but we don't know anything. We're going in essentially blind."

"Regency council came over to see you today. I told them you were sick and didn't want to see anyone. They weren't happy about it, but until the deadline, this is still the royal's house, so they can't come in without permission from the ruler."

I'm going to need to send her on a vacation or buy her something nice when we get this all figured out.

"Thank you, keep them in the dark for as long as you can."

Marci clicked off, and I called Botha's number. In two rings her face was on the space comm.

"Is everything alright, Ma'am? Where are you?"

"Botha, it's a long story, and I don't have much time right now. Are you on Mars?"

"No, we plan on leaving Europa for Triton in a day or two. I should be there in a week, give or take."

"Perfect. Can you position in orbit over Europa?"

"I can ask the captain if he can do it, but I'm sure he will since he's my cousin." Botha chuckled.

"Perfect, I'll reach out again in…" I looked over at Markus who was off screen.

He held up two fingers.

"I'll contact you in two days. Please let your cousin know if he needs to refuel or needs currency for his being in orbit, I will provide it."

"Princess, you sound odd, are you safe?

"I'm safe, other than that, it's day by day."

"Then I'll tell him to orbit, and we'll await your call."

I waved to Botha before clicking off the space comm.

"Who is Botha, and can we trust them?"

I sighed, realizing not everyone knew everything, and before I snapped at Markus for second-guessing my judgement, it dawned on me he didn't know Botha like I did.

"Botha was my mom's doctor. When my mom died, I didn't think about her again, honestly, until recently. She's Martian, and I never saw her after she left. When my father was badly injured the first time, he called Botha in. I was so angry. There was a part of me who believed Botha was responsible for my mom's death. Looking back, I realize she did everything she could, but the little girl in me was still mad at her. I lashed out, not even considering why my father had called her."

Markus got up and handed me a cup of tea from a small pot. "Here, thought you might like this. She was your parents' doctor?"

Taking the cup of tea from Markus, I continued, putting the pieces together while I spoke.

"When my father explained what was going on, it made me realize why he had called Botha in. He called her because he trusted her. He not only trusted her with his life, but he had trusted her with my mom's life as well. The most important people to him were my mom and myself. To trust someone with my mom's life in the face of the unknown, especially someone not from our planet, meant father knew her or at least knew to contact her. When he called her for his own injuries, it meant not only did he trust her with our lives, but he trusted she could keep a secret."

"So, you called her in the event we need a medical person."

"Not just for medical. I saw how she stood when I lashed out at her, not like she expected it, but also like she could take it. She stood like a soldier, like I've seen Tak stand."

"But Tak isn't a soldier."

"No, but he stands like one."

"Interesting observation."

Markus and I turned to the voice. Jasper was leaning against the wall with a cup in his hand.

"How long have been you standing there?"

"Long enough." Jasper walked toward me. Even when he irritated me, I could watch him walking any day, especially if I was his target.

***

After Tahva walked to the bridge, I checked to make sure the girls didn't need anything and went to the kitchen to get something to drink. Tak was still in the kitchen when I walked in.

"How was dinner, Boss?"

"It was delicious as always, thank you. How was having Tahva helping you?"

"At first, I was upset she was here, messing with my stuff. I realized she knew her way around a kitchen, and she was pleasant to work with. Boss, she's full of surprises."

"That's one way to put it."

"Listen, I know you two butt heads sometimes; however, I think she may prove to be an asset. You should give her a chance. I know you don't like asking for help, but you may want to consider it. Please don't think I'm prying; it's an observation."

"Tak, you know you can tell me what I need to hear, even if I don't want to hear it, right? Is there anything else? I want to get back on the bridge in case Markus or Tahva needs me."

"Sounds good. After I'm done cleaning up here, since I have popcorn all over the place, I'll be in my cabin."

Nodding, I took my cup and walked to the bridge. As I got closer, I could hear Tahva talking to someone, but I didn't recognize the voice. When I heard Markus and Tahva talking about someone named Botha, I almost walked in. Tahva started talking about her family, so I quietly leaned against the wall.

Tahva mentioned something about how Tak stood like a soldier, and I felt it was the right time to jump in.

"Interesting observation."

Markus and Tahva looked at me as I walked in.

"How long have you been there?"

"Long enough." I couldn't tell if Tahva was happy to see me or not.

"The reason Tak stands the way he does, and I am sure your friend Botha appears the same way, is because Tak's father was a soldier. He grew up wanting to be like him. You said your friend is a Martian? If she is, she was probably a soldier during the uprising, or her family were soldiers."

"I never thought about it, and I never thought to ask her. I saw her as a doctor and nothing more."

"Remember, Princess, all of us are more than we may appear."

"Thanks for the snotty reply to how I have been treating you."

I put my coffee cup down and my hands up.

"Not at all a snotty reply, I was simply saying sometimes we only see one aspect of a person, when there are multiple. Not all of them are good all the time, some are bad, or maybe not bad, but useful."

"I guess I only look at people superficially. Most of the people I know come in and out of my life without making an impact. I see them at the club, I meet them at an official event, or something along those lines. I don't have much interaction with them. I guess, for me, most people may matter in the grand scheme of things, but also not matter at all. Hopefully I'm making sense."

"It does, and except for a few of our contacts, and you know, our family and friends, it's the same way with us. We interact with clients on a base level. We can't afford to make friends."

"If you went completely legal, could you connect more? Isn't it lonely running all the time?"

"No, because even when you're completely legal, stuff still happens. Look at Jasmine's husband, Raf. Even when you have the best crew, the most honest crew, things still happen. We talked about it and decided to skirt the law sometimes. There's more money in it, and if we're going to die out here anyway, why not die with money for our families."

"That's pragmatic of you."

Tahva's response matched her thoughtful look at what I had said. I meant it. After what happened with Raf, Markus, Tak, and I discussed it, and we decided we would run anything and everything. Everyone dies at some point, and we want to leave something behind for those we care about. It was more than Raf left Jasmine.

"It's the way it is out here in space."

"I guess living on the moon, especially as royalty, I was sheltered. I never left the moon. My life has been protected since I was born, probably even longer."

"Which is why I want to continue protecting you."

"I understand, but this is my choice. What's the plan?"

"First we're picking up the doctor outside of Io. Are you sure she's trustworthy?"

"I would stake my life on it. What I've realized today while talking to Markus is my dad trusted her with his secrets and life, and I know we can do the same."

"We'll pick her up in orbit and get to Triton. Markus, you're in communication with the port master in case something happens, right?"

"Yes, he said there's been minimal movement. He hasn't had eyes on Jasmine yet, but one of his crew did hear them talking about a redhead giving them a bunch of issues."

"Sounds like something Jasmine would do. We'll land at the port, and Tahva, if you want to be part of the plan, tell me now because we could use you."

"I do, but first I need to show you something."

Markus and I watched her leave the bridge.

"What does she have to show us?"

"Boss, she's your intended wife, not mine to figure out."

I rolled my eyes at Markus' comment, but internally I was smiling. She was full of surprises.

CHAPTER 14

I'm not sure how Markus and Jasper will take my surprise. Hopefully well, but some people get weird about it. It was now or never, so I figured I may as well show them. Walking back to the captain's cabin, I thought about when I had found out about my abilities.

My mother had recently died, and I couldn't deal with seeing my father or the doctor who was with her when she took her last breath. We were supposed to live forever. Well, not forever but at least for a long time. Of all the people to contract this disorder, why did it have to be her? The doctor said they had only heard about the disorder in books, it was extremely rare. There was no cure for it because of the rarity. It wasn't fair. I was only 25, I shouldn't have to watch my mother die, hundreds of years before she should. After the doctor declared her dead, I ran. I don't remember exactly where I ran, I knew I didn't want to stop.

When I came back to my senses, I realized I was in the flower garden my mother loved. I laid down among the roses and cried. I don't know how long I was there before I heard Roald calling my name. I kept quiet and laid there, knowing eventually he would find me, but I wasn't going to make it easy for him. As he walked over to where I was lying, I was about to say something to him when I realized he couldn't see me.

"Princess why are your clothes laying here? Where are you?"

At first, I thought he was joking, trying to make me laugh through the pain, but I realized as he looked directly at me, he couldn't see me. I stood and he took a step back. I realized he thought my clothes had stood on their own. Waving my hand in front of his face, there was no recognition I was there.

"Roald can you see me?"

"I don't know how you're doing this, but can you please come out so we can go back inside? Your father is frantic as you have been missing for hours."

"No, I haven't. I've been in this garden for 20 minutes at most." I realized then the sun was setting.

"You have, and your father needs you." Roald kept looking around trying to find me.

"Roald, I'm right in front of you. I'm in the clothes." I closed my eyes and focused on being seen. I heard Roald gasp before I opened my eyes.

"What did you do? You appeared in front of me."

"I don't know. All I know is I laid down in the garden and cried. You came up and couldn't see me. Have you ever heard about someone being able to do this?"

"I've heard of it, but I've never known anyone who could actually do it, or even someone who knew someone who could. We need to tell your father."

I was nervous to tell father, not only because was he dealing with my mother's death, but now I'm a freak. The fact Roald had never seen it meant something, since he knew everything, or at least I thought he did.

Seeing my father sitting at the table broke me. He looked so sad, but I knew I couldn't do anything to help him feel better.

"Roald, do you think we should tell him now? I mean, with everything going on?"

"Yes, he needs to know immediately."

He was so adamant. I resigned myself to the fact not only did we lose my mother, but now my father is going to find out his daughter has something wrong with her.

"King, we need to talk to you about something, and it's important."

"Roald, what could you possibly tell me right now that is more important than what happened to the queen?"

"King, your daughter can disappear."

"She can what?"

"It's true Daddy. I don't know how I did it, but after mother was pronounced dead, I ran outside and found myself in the flower garden. I was laying there, and Roald couldn't see me."

"This isn't possible. We haven't seen this in over 100 years."

"Haven't seen what?" Roald seemed as confused as I was.

"Tahva, you didn't disappear. What you did was reflect light."

"But King, I could see the flowers behind her."

"What does this mean for me?" I was unsure what he meant by reflecting light.

"It means you train to harness this, and you don't tell anyone you can do it. To answer your comment, Roald, yes. It makes our skin like a mirror, so you weren't actually seeing the flowers behind her but a mirror image of flowers around her."

Over the next three years, Roald and my father taught me how to use my talent at will, and I was honestly pretty good at it by now. I almost never used it because if I did, there could be a chance someone would see me and try to take advantage of my abilities.

Opening the cabin door, I went straight to the basket. I opened the small bag I'd found at the bottom of the basket. Marci also knew about my ability, and she had packed something to help us.

Putting on the outfit, I looked at myself in the mirror. It was time to show the guys. I walked back to the bridge, and right before the door opened, I closed my eyes and thought of myself as invisible.

Markus and Jasper stopped talking and looked toward the door. I saw Jasper's brow furrow when he couldn't see anything.

"Markus, did you see anything causing the door to open?"

"Not a thing, Boss."

Making sure I was quiet, I closed the distance between myself and Jasper. When I got close enough, I let my fingers run lightly over his braids, as if a slight wind had come through the bridge. Jasper looked around, not seeing anything.

"Did you feel that, Markus?"

"Feel what, Boss?"

"It felt like it was wind. What the hell is going on?"

Softly chuckling to myself, I walked between Markus and Jasper and focused on making myself appear. Both men gasped as I came back into vision.

"What the hell, Tahva?" Jasper yelled as he took a step back.

"This is what I wanted to show you before we talked about my part of the plan."

"What? Scaring us to death?" Markus leaned forward looking at me.

"I didn't mean to scare you, but I needed to show you what I could do versus telling you."

"Well, you certainly did scare me."

***

When the door opened and no one was there, I was confused. Tahva had said she'd be right back, but it had been a while. I had an itch in the back of my brain telling me I wasn't seeing everything, but I ignored it because my eyes were telling me I was seeing an empty hallway. The itch grew when my hair moved as though a short breeze had come through, but it didn't appear Markus had felt it. It wasn't until Tahva appeared in between Markus and me, when I realized what the itch had been.

I knew something wasn't quite right, but I didn't know what. Having walked the hallway thousands of times, I could walk these halls with my eyes closed. There was something off about the hallway. Now I realize I wasn't seeing the hallway behind Tahva, but what the sides of the hall looked like. She had been able to distort our view.

Looking back at Tahva, I realized she was wearing a body suit going from the hood covering her hair to her feet.

"I have an ability which allows me to reflect light." It was like Tahva knew what I was going to ask. "This outfit reflects light on its own, so when I fade away, it fades away with me. If I was wearing something else, you'd be able to see my clothes, but not me."

"Interesting, I haven't heard of an Ioian being able to reflect light. Is it a rare ability?"

Tahva paused before answering.

"Tahva, Markus and I won't tell anyone if it's something you're worried about."

"Thank you, and honestly yes, it is something I was nervous about telling you. While what I can do is technically an Ioian trait, there hasn't been another with my ability in over 100 years. At least not that we know of."

"Wow, probably why we've never heard of it. Do you know how you came about having it?"

"After we discovered I could do it, we started looking into the history of the ability." Tahva explained how she found out she could do it on the same day her mother died.

"So, you started training on how to use it better?"

"Yes, Roald and my father did a lot of research into the ability, and we discovered the last person who could do it, at least documented, was a relative of my mother's. Interestingly enough, her relative also had the same rare condition my mother had. My father thinks I got the ability from her. We also think the disorder responsible for killing my mother may also be heredity."

"Wait. Do you have it?"

"I'm a carrier for it. I only have half of my mother's genetics, so if I had children with someone who was distantly related to my mother, our children could have it."

"Were your mother's parents related somehow?"

"Yes, it appears no one knew at the time, but they were 10th cousins, and they happened to both be carriers. Which is one of the reasons why I never wanted to have children. Well, I guess I never even wanted to get married."

It was all starting to make sense why Tahva wasn't already married and why she went with a matchmaker who looked all over the solar system. It wasn't the time or place to ask her about her thoughts on children right now, especially as we were getting ready to possibly put our lives on the line. I heard Markus clear his throat.

"Boss, we are close to Io. We need to get the doctor on board and our plan finalized."

"Tahva, do you want to contact the doctor to let her know we're going to make a spacebridge in 20 minutes with her ship? Before you do, how many people know about your ability?"

"My father and Roald obviously. Marci does as well, and she created this outfit for me. Other than them, I don't think anyone else knows. We made sure to keep it a secret from the regency council because my father believed they would use it for their own purposes. I never even told any of the men I've dated, mostly because those relationships never lasted more than a month or two."

"Does the doctor know?" I asked her. I needed to know who I could trust with this secret.

"I don't think so, but she is someone who could be trusted with it."

"Give her a call, and let's get this plan worked out with her on board."

"Sounds good."

I watched Tahva go to the comm system to call the doctor. I walked over to Markus and lowered my voice.

"Do you think she can handle this?"

"I don't know, Boss, but she's going to be part of it. There's no way you're going to stop her."

"I know but I'm worried about her. She seems strong but also naïve, you know?"

"Boss, I don't think she's as naïve as she seems, and her skills could benefit us, especially to get eyes on Jasmine."

"I know but I don't want to put her in danger."

"You can't protect us forever. Fate will decide our future. If you push her, you'll lose her."

"I know you're right, Markus, but I still don't like it."

"Like with other parts of life, you don't have to like everything for it to work."

"But I can try, Markus, I can try."

Tahva came back over to let us know Botha was waiting for us and gave us the coordinates for where to meet her.

"Thank you, Markus. Can you get Botha on board while Tahva and I arrange a place for her to sleep during our stay?"

"Will do." He turned toward the console to make the necessary calculations.

"Let's go talk to everyone. When Botha gets on board, we'll have a meeting with Tak, Markus, Cynthia, you, Botha, and me, and we'll get a plan finalized."

"Why Cynthia? If you don't mind me asking."

"Ask away, you're a part of this. Cynthia needs to know for two reasons. The first is she will be with the girls, and if something goes bad, she needs to know what to do. The second reason is, like you, she has some abilities. Her abilities aren't exactly like yours though, they were more taught throughout her life."

"That makes sense. I think if Cynthia's fine with it, we can put the girls with her and put Botha in the room the girls were in."

"How about we move Cynthia to the girl's cabin and put Botha in Cynthia's cabin? I only say it because Chad and Chloe are in there with the girls, and I don't want Botha to deal with quokka fur."

"Since I'm sure Botha has never seen a quokka before, it's probably a good idea. Do I have time to change?"

"Yeah, I'll go back to the bridge. Let me know if you need anything."

"Thank you, and I will." Tahva turned and walked into my cabin. Or I guess, right now, it was *our* cabin. I knew how I felt about sharing but not how she felt about sharing a cabin with me. Sometimes she ran cold like she couldn't stand to be in my presence, and other times she acted like she actually wanted to be around me. I knew we needed to sit down and talk, but with everything going on, there didn't seem to be the time. I hope by rescuing Jasmine, we would both make it out and have time to focus on us and if there was anything between us.

***

When I heard Jasper walk away from the door, I leaned against it. What was I doing? I was so conflicted. I wanted to jump into his arms and have him hold me, but I also knew there hadn't been a time or place for it so far. I'd thought by offering to stay in his cabin he would realize I wanted to be with him. But instead, he seemed bothered I'd offered. Was marrying this man who traveled and put himself in harm's way the type of life I wanted to live? Did I even want to be married? I know I did, and I've always wanted to be married. I also always worried about marrying an Ioian because of the genetic disorder my mother had. I couldn't condemn a child to an early death.

Shaking my head, I quickly changed knowing Botha would be on the ship soon. Walking out wearing a casual outfit, I heard the spacebridge engage. I followed Tak and Jasper to the door as Botha walked through. Her shock at seeing me on a ship was genuine as I went and hugged her.

"Thank you for agreeing to come along."

"I have no idea what I signed up for, but you know how I feel about your family, so when you call, I answer."

"We'll get you settled in, and we'll have a meeting about what's going on and what the plan is after."

"If you can direct me to some food first, I'll be happy. My cousin's cooking isn't great."

Laughing, I introduced her to Tak, and he took her to the kitchen to make her something to eat. As they walked away, I asked Jasper if he'd talked to Cynthia about rooming with the girls. He said he'd stopped by on his way to the bridge to let her know and she didn't mind.

"Tahva, if you want to grab something to eat, we'll have the meeting in about ten minutes, or whenever Tak is finished making food for Botha."

"Thank you, I think I will." I walked to the kitchen.

Walking into the kitchen, I could smell Tak's cooking. "Tak, can you make me some of whatever you're making for Botha please?"

"Will do, Ma'am."

"I've never heard of you leaving Io. What's going on?" Botha asked after she placed her teacup back on the table.

"Long story short, my father had to go into hiding. I was to become queen but couldn't without being married. Father thought I should go to a matchmaker. I did and got matched with Jasper. He's the tall red-haired captain you met at the bridge door. I was almost killed at the club, his sister was kidnapped, and we went to earth to get her daughters. Oh, and we found out where she was being held, so we picked you up on our way there."

"I can't wait to hear the long story because it hasn't been long since I saw you last." Botha and I talked about other things until Tak brought us our food.

"This looks good, Tak, thank you." I started to eat.

Botha went straight to the food and nodded her approval.

"I'm glad you like it. I want to check something out in the armory before we have our meeting. If there's anything else you need, please let me know."

Finally taking a break from eating, Botha stopped Tak. "I served in the Martian military. Can I look at the armory following our meeting?"

Tak's eyes lit up at Botha's words.

"Of course you can. I can take you there right after the meeting. We even have some Martian weapons on board you might like." Tak left to go manage his business.

"So, two Humans and a Titan on one ship? That sounds like the beginning of a bad joke."

"Well technically, it's five Humans, a Titan, a Martian, and an Ioian." We laughed as we talked about mundane things while finishing our food.

"Leave the plates here, and I'll clean up later."

"You wash dishes?"

"Botha, there's a lot about me you don't know." I winked at her as we walked to the bridge. It was going to be a tight fit with everyone in there, but I doubted the meeting would be long.

As I entered, I noticed everyone was there except Jasper and Markus.

Turning to Cynthia, I asked how the girls were doing.

"They're fine. They're cuddled in bed with Chad and Chloe watching a show on their screen. I doubt they even realized I was leaving."

"Ahh to be young," Botha chimed in.

"What are you talking about? I lay in bed and watch shows, and I'm not young."

"But you're a princess. Which means you get to do what you want, when you want."

"I wish. Ask the captain when he comes in."

"Ask the captain what?" Jasper smirked as he took his seat. I hadn't noticed the door open when Markus and Jasper came in.

"Nothing, we were talking about you." Cynthia covered for me.

I nodded to her.

"I'm sure you were. Since we're all here, let's start the planning meeting. Markus can you bring us up to speed?"

"Sure thing, Boss."

***

This was the second time I'd caught Tahva talking about me. In a manner of speaking, at least. I could stand there and listen to her talk forever, but it won't get Jasmine back.

I snuck glances at her and Botha while Markus was giving the rundown of what had happened, where we were going, and what we knew. After Markus was finished, I spoke up.

"Botha, you're here because Tahva trusts you, and because we may need a doctor. Either for Jasmine, as we don't know what condition she is in, or for one of us depending on the situation. If you want out, let us know now, and we can drop you off on Triton before we start the rescue mission."

"No, I'm absolutely in. Well, as long as I can check out the armory."

Laughing, I looked at Tak. "As long as Tak is okay with you touching his things, I'm don't care. We'll need all hands-on deck."

"I don't have a problem with it, Boss, and she may be able to help us with some of the Martian weapons we've picked up."

"You heard the man. You're good to go, don't lose anything."

"I would never, but I'll also need a triage kit."

I already liked Botha as she didn't blink at what we may be walking into. I think she could be a good addition to the team if she wanted to be. Expanding the crew was a matter for another day.

"Tak can set you up with one of those as well. Now we can talk about the actual plan. Here's what I'm thinking and let me know what you think." I looked over at Tahva and she nodded.

I knew she was safe with Botha and Tak knowing about what she could do. I was impressed, as well as humbled, that she would expose her abilities to essential strangers to save Jasmine. I needed to talk to her about how I felt, but no time had seemed right for it.

"When we arrive in the spaceport, they're holding Jasmine in one of the hangars. The port master has eyes on the hangar, and he is to alert us of any movement before we get there. Tahva will take point."

Tak and Botha spoke up at the same time, "But Jasper, she's a Princ-"

Before I could say anything, Tahva disappeared. Flair for the dramatic I guess, since I could have just told them.

"Yes, I'm still here, and yes, I am, for lack of better term, invisible. This is why I'm going in first."

I continued before Tak or Botha could say anything else. "Now that we have everything out in the open, can we continue going over the plan?" I looked around and everyone nodded.

"Tak will be the first off the ship.

Once Tak makes sure it's clear, Tahva will go into the building first. When she can get a good look at what's happening inside the hangar, she'll come out and quickly brief us.

As soon as we know what to expect, Markus, myself, and Tak will head in. Botha will follow if needed and cover our backs.

As of right now, Cynthia will be on the ship with the girls as well as our comms.

The minute anyone gets eyes on Jasmine, you are to grab her and get her back to the ship. Once we know she's safe, the rest of us are to return to the ship. If something happens and one of us gets taken down, your number one priority is to get Jasmine, Cynthia, the girls, and Tahva to safety.

Does everyone understand?"

"Jasper, what am I supposed to be doing after I give you the information?"

"You're to stay on the ship with Cynthia and the girls."

"I don't think so. You're not going to use my skills and then hide me away like I'm some fragile flower."

I could see the rest of the group look between Tahva and me, and I didn't have the time to fight with her right now.

"Listen, you will stay on the ship, and we'll talk about this later. Do you understand?"

Tahva crossed her arms, but she agreed with a sharp nod of her head. I knew we would talk about it later, but for right now, I had to get everything straight with everyone else. This could be dangerous, and I didn't want to lose anyone, especially Jasmine. I also wanted to find out who had done this, and I wanted to make them pay. No one messed with my family. I was trying to figure out the connection. Once everyone goes to sleep, I'd have Tak and Markus meet with me, and we could try to figure out if there was one.

"Once Jasmine and Tahva are back on the ship, you have three minutes to make it to the ship before we take-off. Do you understand? Cynthia knows how to fly the ship if necessary."

"No, we can wait for you," Tahva objected.

"No, you, Jasmine, the girls, Cynthia, and the ship are more important. If anything happens, we can lay low and catch a ride on another ship to Io. You five are to get there and be protected. Tahva, they can be protected no matter what on Io, right?"

Tahva stood a little taller. "Yes, without a doubt they'll be protected with my life as well as the life of my house."

"Tahva, if something happens to you, will they still take them in?"

"Absolutely. Cynthia, as you are staying on board, if you must, there is a charm in the basket in the captain's cabin. Take the charm and present it to the port master at Io. He'll know what to do if you give that to him."

"Does anyone have any questions? We're 36 hours from Triton, and I want everyone to be well rested and ready."

No one spoke up.

"Then, get some food, get some sleep. Tak, Markus, can I talk to you two?"

Everyone but Tak, Markus, and Tahva left the bridge.

"Do you need me, or can I go get some sleep?" The attitude Tahva had when we first met was back.

"You can go to sleep. I'll be there in a while to catch some sleep after you wake up."

"Fine, whatever." She stormed off the bridge.

"Damn boss, you screwed up." Markus shook his head.

"It's never the right thing. I can't win, but it isn't why I wanted to talk to you."

"What's up?"

"There's something bothering me. We've never had someone go after one of our family members before. We haven't had many issues other than the one time on Triton."

"Yeah, true."

"Why now? What's changed? We had the client we took to Triton and the material shipment to Europa. What am I missing?"

"From my side, everything has been the same. There's been no strange people spending too long watching us, nothing out of the ordinary for the type of missions we've had."

I figured he was going to say what he did. I know if something was different, he would've let me know.

"Markus, do you have any insight?"

"Both missions were new clients, but they came highly recommended by previous clients. The Triton to Europa was a quasi-government contract, so it's probably on the up and up. The client we took out to Triton was client transport. Someone else paid for him., we got paid half up front and half when he was dropped off."

"Nothing unusual about the trips. What else can you think of? It's on the tip of my tongue, but I can't figure it out."

"I don't know Jasper, maybe it's a combination of things, you know? Maybe they aren't connected," Markus thought out loud.

"Maybe, but you know when things don't feel right, they usually aren't. We need to make sure to be careful."

"Copy, Boss." Tak moved toward the door.

"Get some rest. I'll stay on the bridge. In 6 hours can you come relieve me, Markus?"

"Will do." Markus left the bridge to sleep.

For the next six hours, I kept rerunning the plan in my head, trying to figure out why this was all happening and thinking about Tahva. No matter what else I thought about, it always came back to Tahva. It was weird to not know someone and in such a short amount of time to not be able to stop thinking about them. I didn't know what the future would hold. Honestly, I wanted us to all get out of Triton in one piece.

I could feel my body shutting down and couldn't remember the last time I got more than a couple hours of sleep in the captain's chair. When Markus came to relieve me, I would need to argue with Tahva about her staying on the ship. I don't understand why it's so hard for her to listen. I was trying to protect her. I knew she thought I didn't think she could protect herself, but I knew she could. I didn't want her to have to. I felt myself falling asleep at the same time Markus came in with a cup of coffee.

"Where's mine?"

"In the kitchen later after you wake up. We're less than a day out from Triton, and you need to get some sleep. Did you come up with anything while you were up here?"

"Nothing, I kept rolling everything around in my head, but nothing connected."

"I'll think about it while I'm here doing nothing. Now go get some sleep."

"Will do."

I hoped Tahva was already awake. I didn't want to wake her, but I also didn't want to get into an argument right now. I wanted to sleep, and hopefully, while I did, something would come to me. I hated not knowing what I was getting into, and I was worried about my crew. I kept thinking about it as I went to my cabin.

When I got to the cabin, I was thankful I had the smooth-glide doors put in because as I entered, I realized Tahva was still asleep. Not wanting to wake her, I quietly opened the closet and pulled down a blanket and pillow. Laying it on the floor, I moved the chair so I could stretch out.

"You can come up onto the bed."

"I didn't wake you, did I?"

"Yes, you did, but I'll go back to sleep. Now come up here; you shouldn't be on the floor."

"Are you sure?"

"Jasper, I'm not going to tell you again." It sounded like she turned over and went back to sleep.

Smiling, I laid down as close to the edge as I could. Before I knew it, sleep overtook me.

CHAPTER 15

I don't know why I invited Jasper up to the bed, but it was out of my mouth before I realized what I was saying. There was a part of me wanting him to hold me. The other part, though, was still mad at him for thinking I couldn't protect or handle myself. I could handle myself, and I'll show him when we get to Triton.

As he got into bed, I kept my face turned away. I knew he was going to sleep on the edge, but what I would have given for him to wrap me in his arms. His breathing slowed as I laid there, and I knew he was asleep. I laid there for a while until I knew he was deep asleep.

I carefully sat up and moved to the edge of the bed before getting off, doing my best not to wake him. I quietly opened the door and stepped out, looking back at the sleeping Jasper. His brow was furrowed like he was having a nightmare, and while I wanted to ease his burdens, I know the best I could do is to help them once we get on the planet.

Stretching, I walked into the kitchen to get something to eat. Tak was sitting at the table drinking what smelled like tea. I have a pretty good sense of smell, and my mom loved tea. It soothed a part of me when someone was drinking it.

"Good morning, Princess." Tak raised his cup to me.

"Do you have any more tea? Also, please stop calling me princess, not only because right now I'm on a spaceship, but also because I hate everyone calling me princess. I have a name, one my mother and father gave me."

"Okay, Tahva, I won't call you princess anymore unless it's a formal setting on Io. Better?"

"I appreciate it. What do you think's going to happen once we get to Triton?" I asked as he stood to get my tea.

Turning around with my cup in his hand, his eyes were sad but strong. "Honestly, I hope it's a simple in and out. I don't like seeing people get hurt, even bad people."

I put my hand on his shoulder while I took the cup of tea with the other. "I understand. I hate seeing people get hurt, but I also realize sometimes it's a necessary evil, especially if those people are hurting someone we care about."

"True Pr... I mean, Tahva. I protect my family and cook food."

"You are always welcome to cook for me, Tak, and I hope you consider me family. If not now, at some point in the future. I do care about your captain." The tea tasted better than any tea I'd had since my mother died.

"Did you put something in this? It's incredible." I looked between the tea and Tak.

"No, it's tea from Io. I don't think it's special or anything. Before we left for Earth, Jasper made sure I picked up some local teas for you."

He did what? Even though we were fighting at the time? He has more layers than I gave him credit for. No wonder his crew follows him everywhere.

Not wanting to get too deep inside my head about Jasper or my feelings toward him, I thanked Tak.

"I'm going to the bridge. If Jasper wakes up, please let him know where I am."

With a small smirk, Tak bowed his head. "Of course, Tahva."

As I walked out, he was removing vegetables from the cabinet, whistling a tune. I smiled as I made my way to the bridge.

***

"Did you sleep well, Tahva? Jasper didn't wake you, did he?"

"No, Markus, I was already awake when he came to the room." What was a little white lie?

"I'm glad. He can be an absolute dolt when it comes to people sleeping. I know from personal experience." Markus chuckled.

"I don't see coffee or anything. Do you want me to go get you something?" I didn't know how long Markus had been at the bridge, but I had a desire to help him. Not just him but the rest of the ship's current inhabitants, too. I even want to help Jasmine, and she may hate me for being with and not with her brother.

"A coffee would be great." Looking at his watch, and back at the screen, he continued, "Can you also let Tak know we need to eat soon because we are about 3 hours from Triton, and I want to make sure he has time to prepare."

"I can. Do you want me to wake everyone up?" I asked as I walked off the bridge.

"No, I'll announce it when Tak lets me know the food is ready. It isn't like our ship is huge."

"Gotcha, so one coffee and a message for Tak. I'll be back with it soon." I hurried off to let Tak know and to get Markus' coffee. Heading to the kitchen, I heard Cynthia talking to the girls.

"Time to get dressed for breakfast, girls. Juju what's wrong?"

Through the sniffles, I heard her sister tell Cynthia Juju was worried about their mom.

"Girls, your uncle is going to bring your mom home soon. We need to take a small trip somewhere, and then she'll be with us."

"Will we go home after?"

I realized I didn't want them to leave because if they did, Jasper may also leave. I wasn't ready for him to be out of my life. I realized I had been standing there while Cynthia talked to the girls.

Feeling insecure, I rushed to the kitchen. It smelled so good, like baked goods but not baked. I think it was what they called pancakes, but I didn't know for sure since I'd never had them before.

"Tak, Markus wanted me to let you know we are only three hours from Triton, and he wanted to make sure you had enough time after cooking to get ready. Can I get a cup of coffee for him?"

Tak handed me a cup of coffee he had waiting for me. "Let him know the food will be done in about 20 minutes." He turned back to what he was cooking.

As I walked back to the bridge, Cynthia and the girls were heading to the kitchen to eat.

"Hi Princess, did you sleep well?" Jannie asked me as she held her sister's hand.

"I did, Jannie, thank you for asking. Did you sleep well?"

"Aunt Cynthia read us a book, and after Juju was asleep, she stayed up with me a little longer and read another whole chapter. She said it was a little too scary for Juju, but I didn't think it was scary at all."

I looked over Jannie's head and smiled at Cynthia who was shaking her head.

"I'm glad you didn't think it scary. Did you know Tak is cooking right now?" I lifted a cup. "And I have to get this to Markus because he's been working hard on the bridge."

Jannie started hopping from foot to foot. "Aunt Cynthia, I want to help Tak. He said I could, and we have to hurry before he's done."

"Okay, okay, Jannie. We can go help Tak."

I turned back toward the bridge, listening to Jannie continue telling Cynthia about how she was going to help Tak. Tak was particular with his kitchen, so I'm sure he'll be pleased having a child in there 'helping'. I noticed Tak did seem to have a soft spot for the girls though, so who knows.

"Here's your coffee, Markus. Tak said it'll be ready in about 20 minutes if you wanted to announce over the speaker breakfast is almost ready. Do you want me to wake Jasper?"

Markus was looking at a map. When I walked closer, I could tell it was the airfield on Triton. One of the things I knew from years of schooling growing up, was to look at the airfields from other locations. My father insisted the royal family knew how to read the maps and could fly to any location if we needed to. I loved ships and airfields and even offered to help him design one on the property if he ever wanted to have one. I never left the planet, but it had always interested me.

"Thank you, and yes, can you wake him up? After we eat, we need to have another meeting once we're about an hour out. I want to ensure everything is good before we land. I have a feeling we may not come in under the radar, and I don't want it to go sideways."

Nodding, I left the bridge to make my way back to the captain's room. I walked through the door with my eyes on the floor. As I raised my head to wake Jasper, I realized he was already awake. Not only was he awake, but he was shirtless and turned away from me. My mind was conflicted. I wanted to keep watching him get ready, but on the other hand, I wanted him to know I was there. There was also a small part of me wanting to run my hands up and down his bare back. As much as we fought, it was undeniable. I was attracted to him, but was he attracted to me?

***

I knew someone had come in, and when they didn't immediately announce themselves, I figured it was Tahva. I didn't say anything but kept getting ready. I found braiding my hair to be easier without my hair sticking to a shirt. This time, I was weaving a single bead onto the braid. I may have taken longer than normal knowing Tahva was watching. Figuring I had given her enough of a show, I turned around.

Her eyes widened as she ogled my chest. I smirked as her cheeks took on a rosy hue.

"Did you need something?"

Clearing her throat, she stuttered before speaking, "Um, yeah, Markus said to let you know breakfast is almost ready, and when we are one hour out from Triton, we're going to have another meeting regarding what's going to happen once we land. He thinks we won't go unnoticed."

"Sounds good. Let me finish up, and I'll meet you in the kitchen." I turned to grab my shirt and put it on, giving Tahva another view of my back. I wasn't vain, but it was nice to hear her gasp as I flexed my shoulders to put my shirt on.

I headed to the kitchen. The minute I stepped out of the bedroom I could smell breakfast from the kitchen. While the smell was the first thing I noticed, I also heard the giggles of the two girls and Cynthia laughing at whatever someone had said. Even with everything going on, it was still nice to hear all of them laughing, and I couldn't help but smile.

I didn't know what was going to happen in the next 24 hours, but I knew I had to not only protect my family, but also Tahva and my crew. It was my job as captain to make sure everyone who left the ship made it back to the ship in one piece, if possible, and I was going to do everything I could to make sure everyone left Triton. Right now, I couldn't focus on the future; I had to shake it off and get ready for Triton.

"Uncle Jasper!"

"Uncle Jasper!"

Both girls ran up to me and jumped up into my arms.

"Hi girls, we need to eat, alright? Then Uncle Markus and I are going to get your mom."

"Uncle Jasper, I even helped Tak with breakfast! I made some of it all by myself."

"Jannie, you did? All by yourself?" I looked up at Tak and saw him winking.

"Yes, all by myself. I made the syrup."

"I can't wait. Did everyone hear? Jannie made the syrup, so make sure you get some."

Jannie's smile lit up the kitchen as Tak handed everyone their plates.

"On your plates you have Dutch babies, which is a mix between a pancake and a crepe. On the plates in the center of the table, there are eggs and bacon. I cooked the bacon well done because I know most of you like it crispy. For the eggs I made a variety of styles. I know Markus likes over easy, and Jasper likes them scrambled, but I wasn't sure what everyone else likes. There's also butter and syrup. As you already know, Jannie made the syrup, and it's from a fruit only found on Io, Tahva."

"It was all my idea, Tahva. I asked Tak if he had anything from your moon."

Tahva hugged Jannie, and my heart ached.

"Thank you so much. This means so much to me."

Jannie's smile was huge when she sat back down in her chair.

"Before we start eating, I wanted to remind Markus, Tak, Cynthia, and Tahva about our meeting when we are an hour outside of Triton to finalize plans. I need everyone to be ready before then. Any questions?"

When no one said anything, I continued. "Let's eat." I didn't have to say it twice.

***

He was so sweet when it came to the girls. I could see how he would be a great parent if he chose to have children someday. Obviously, not with me since I don't want to have kids. I didn't even know if Humans and Ioians could even have kids together. Not that I should be thinking about it at all at this time or place.

We were getting close to Triton, so I needed to have my mind straight to help rescue Jasmine. I realized I didn't want to help her to prove Jasper wrong. Originally, I was, but now I want to make sure those two little girls got their mom back and Jasper got his sister

161

back. It didn't matter what happened to me or what happened between Jasper and me. I needed to make sure Jasmine was back with her girls.

Shaking my head, I ate what I could. Tak was such a good cook. I wonder if I could get him to join my staff when all of this was over. I could see he enjoyed space, so I doubt he'd want to. I finished eating, stood and stretched, wincing as I did.

"Are you sore? Where are you going? Don't forget we have a meeting," Jasper spoke through a mouthful of food.

"One thing at a time. I'm sore, but I'll be okay. As to where I'm going, I'll be in our room for a bit, and then I'll be at the meeting." Chuckling to myself, I left and went toward the room.

I heard steps coming up fast behind me, so I turned right as I got to the door. "Jasper, what are you doing? You need to be eating." I walked into the room.

"Did you sleep well? I'm sorry if I kept you up last night."

"It wasn't you at all. I didn't sleep well because I'm worried about everything I can't control but wish I could. Do you know what I mean?"

Jasper put his hands on my hips. "I know exactly what you mean. Every time we go on a job or a mission, I worry about what's going to happen to my crew and to my ship. I worry about making it home to Jasmine and the girls. Now I worry about you and making sure you're safe."

"Why me? We barely know each other. I'm nothing more than a spoiled princess."

"You may be a spoiled princess, but you've done more for me and my family than anyone else not currently on this ship."

I didn't know what I was doing, but I placed my arms around his neck and kissed him. It felt right as he pulled me closer. Our bodies fit together perfectly. I pulled back and smiled. Jasper returned my smile.

"Here I'm thinking we should stay in the room and worry about things later. I know it isn't really an option, but it would be nice, wouldn't it?"

Jasper kissed my forehead before smiling back. "I agree with you, but yes, we have to go save my sister, and we can talk more about us later."

"Sounds good. Don't get yourself hurt because it's hard for me to take care of sick or injured people, do you understand?"

"Crystal, Princess." We left the room to meet about what we were going to be facing in about an hour.

***

I can't believe she kissed me. I was a nothing. A Human pirate who owned a spaceship. She was the princess of an entire moon. An influential one according to Markus' research. I wanted to stay in the room with her, but I knew we had a mission, and Jasmine needed to be my priority. Before the meeting started, I snuck peeks at Tahva as the rest of the group came in from the kitchen. She was much stronger than I gave her credit for. Under her spoiled exterior, was a fighter. Because of her, I wanted to be a fighter, and to be stronger, when I was scared to death. I was scared we would get there too late.

Taking a deep breath, I focused on the people around me. They were my crew from all over the solar system, and we were a family.

"We're less than an hour outside of Triton, and we need to be right about this. Markus, can you share with us what you've learned?

163

Have you gotten any new info since our last meeting?" I looked over at Markus as he stood.

"Jasmine's being held at hangar 7. As you can see from the map, it's at the back of the airfield where there are less patrols. This means if we get into deep trouble, we aren't going to have help for a while. I have the port master on notice, and he knows we're planning on coming in unannounced and leaving the same way. He was leery of it, but Tahva spoke to him, and he's fine now, right?"

"Yes, I reminded him of a favor he owes my father. Him looking the other way won't even come close to repaying the favor, but it does put him in a good light with the future royal family of Io."

I couldn't help but notice Tahva looking at me when she said it.

Wait, does she want me to stay with her? Be her king? Or consort? Or whatever they call it on Io.

Markus nodded and continued after Tahva finished. "Once again, it pays to have royalty on board. Our goal is minimal damage and minimal exposure. I think it would be in our best interest to keep this as under the radar as we can. Right, Jasper?"

"You're right. The original plan was for Tahva to scope things out and update us first, and then Tak would go in. Instead, I think Tak should go in first. I'm not a huge fan of her going before him. It's too dangerous." I looked at Tahva.

"I think I should go in first. I'm much quieter than Tak with all his weaponry." Tahva waited for me to argue.

"Captain, if I may?"

"What is it, Markus?"

"I actually think Tahva should go in with her suit before Tak goes to determine where Jasmine is being held like we'd originally planned. With her suit, she can get in quietly."

"I understand, Captain, but we've seen what she can do. I think her going in undetected would be best. In fact, once she finds where Jasmine is, we can be a distraction to get them away from where they're holding her, and Tahva can get her out and back to the ship. I think it's a good idea."

"As much as I don't like the plan, Markus is right. It's the best plan to get in get out quietly," Jasper replied.

"Tahva, you know what to do, right?" I wanted to reach out to her and tell her I would protect her.

"Yup, I get it. Get Jasmine, get out. Easy peasy." Tahva was way too excited to be involved.

"Don't get too arrogant. We want everyone to get back to the ship safely."

"I won't, I promise I'll be careful."

"Once we get Jasmine, unless Botha had to get off the ship to cover us, she will check everyone out. Tak will be the last onto the ship. Cythnia will be at the commands, and as soon as Tak is on board, we will lift-off. I want everyone to gather in the kitchen except for Tak so if we have any unwanted occupants or there is a firefight, only Tak is exposed. Does everyone understand?"

All through the room, people were nodding. It was somber to think if something went sideways, this could be one of the last times I worked with them.

"Listen, I don't want to be sentimental, but this could be a bad fight. We don't know who's there, how many, or anything. I know I will not be leaving Triton without my sister. I can't ask you all to do the same, but please be careful, and if we can get her on board, and I'm not back, take-off without me. Do you understand?"

I could tell Tak and Markus wanted to argue with me. I could also see Tahva getting ready to argue.

"Stop, I'm the captain of this ship, and if I tell you to leave, you leave. Do you understand me?"

This time, no one tried to argue with me. I hoped it didn't come to that, but I wanted to make sure Jasmine, the girls, and Tahva were safe. I also knew Tahva would take care of Jasmine and the girls if it came down to it.

"Markus, anything else?"

"The only thing left is where are we going once we get Jasmine? I don't want to go back to Earth because whoever took her may come looking for us there. Does anyone have suggestions?"

I was the first to chime in. "I don't think we should go back to Io right away either."

"Wait, why not? My place is perfectly safe."

"No offense, Tahva, but with your father's assassination attempt and the shooting at the club, they may still try to come after you. We don't know who or why they took Jasmine, and it could be all tied in together."

"Why would anyone go from my father, to me, to your sister? That doesn't make sense. It was probably something you did, yourself." Tahva sat back with her arms crossed and an attitude.

"Probably, but I still don't want to risk it. Tak, could we go to Titan?"

"We could, but I haven't been home since I left. Suddenly appearing after all this time could cause some waves. Mom will love seeing me though." Tak smiled sadly. *I need to remember to take him home more often.*

"Titan, Triton, Io, and Earth are out. Where else is there?"

"What about Europa?" Tahva spoke up.

"Why Europa?"

"It isn't highly habitable, but Io is spending a lot of money there to help build it up, so no one would look twice at the Princess of Io showing up."

"You don't think they'll let your regency council know?"

Tahva scoffed. "If anything, they'll make sure the regency council doesn't know. There are some on the council who don't want Io to support Europa and were fighting with my dad regarding sending money and supplies there. If I show support for the construction, which I do support, they'll welcome us with open arms."

"It sounds good to me, Captain. We can lay low for a little while afterwards." Markus chimed in.

It sounded good, but it also got my mind whirling about if the situation with Europa had caused some of the issues we are facing. *I wonder if the argument Tahva's father had with the regency council was one of the reasons he was injured and now on the run.*

"It's settled. Markus, how long before we enter Triton's atmosphere?" I paced while he looked at the screens. I needed to be doing something, anything, to keep my mind off the fact we were walking into something we don't have all the information for. We always had a plan, double checked usually. This time, we were essentially blind, and I didn't like it.

"Captain, we're ten minutes from atmosphere."

"Any other questions before we get into positions? Tak, you ready?"

"Yes, Captain. I'm going to the armory now. I'll be ready."

"I'm ready too, Jasper. I just need to get on my suit." Tahva stood, heading to change.

"Cynthia? Botha?"

"I'm ready." Cythnia replied.

"I'm ready as well in case we have injuries. However, I didn't see a medical bay on this ship."

"We don't have one, Botha. Use the armory if needed; it's big enough for all of us in case—"

"Jasper, please don't worry about medical. If need be, I can handle everyone. I did it before in war, so I can do it for what? Four people going in?" Botha placed her hand on my shoulder.

"Thank you, Botha. I'm sorry I brought you into this." I didn't know her well, and I felt bad because she could be at risk as well.

"I didn't come for you, I came for Tahva, and after all her family has gone through and done for me, I will follow her anywhere." Botha looked at Tahva.

I could tell Tahva wanted to say something, but we didn't have time. Before I could say anything, Markus spoke up.

"We are five minutes away. We need to get ready."

"Alright, Let's go. I'll be in the loading bay with Tak. Tahva, get dressed and meet me there. Cythnia, the minute we land, you'll be on the bridge. Botha will be at the loading dock ready to back us up if we need it. Do you think the girls will be good in their room?"

"Yeah, I put on a show, and they'll lay there with the quokka." Cynthia replied as she stood.

Everyone except Markus and Cythnia left the bridge. Tahva brushed her hand against my arm as she left.

"Markus, I'm worried. I can't let anything happen to you all. You're my family."

Markus came closer. "Captain, we're in this together. If we fall, we all fall, but we won't. With the new plan, I think we have a good chance of getting in and out with no one noticing until it's too late."

"I hope you're right." I walked off the bridge toward the loading bay. I had to trust my crew would be safe and work together as we have always done so many times before.

As I followed, I realized I was heading into, what could be, a battle with people I trust. I even trusted Tahva to do what she needed to do to protect herself and my sister. Still, watching Tahva walk into the building was one of the scariest things I had ever done. I knew I had to trust her, but it wasn't just her, but also my sister who was in danger.

CHAPTER 16

I worry about Jasper. He's carrying too much on his shoulders. As I went back to the room, I thought about how he was taking everything on himself when he had a great crew around him. I wonder if he did this with every job or if it's because it was his sister. I couldn't stop thinking about Jasper as I changed into my suit. I wonder what my dad would think about what I was doing. I had always been the girly girl. Not wanting to get involved with politics or anything taking away from my fun. Little did he know I had paid attention, maybe not as much as I should have, but I did pay attention.

Leaving the loading bay in my suit, I felt strong and capable. I wanted to feel this way all the time. It felt great knowing I was on a ship with people who believed I could do anything I said I could do. It felt good, not something I'd felt often on Io where people tip-toed around me as the future queen. It was annoying at times, and I think it's why I acted like the dumb raver and constant party girl.

"I'm ready."

"Good, we're about to land. Remember, Tak will be first out the door and then you."

"Got it."

It wasn't long before I felt the ship slowing and a slight bump as we landed. I had to hand it to Markus; he could fly this thing. I wasn't going to tell Jasper, but I thought Markus was a better pilot than he was. *I'm sure Jasper already knew he wasn't as good as Markus*, I thought. Chuckling to myself, I waited for Tak to leave the ship.

"Tahva, can I talk to you for a second?" Jasper approached as the door was opening, and Tak was gearing up.

"Sure, everything okay?"

"Please be careful. We don't know what we're going to find in there, and I don't want anything to happen to you."

"Why? Because you care about me?"

"Yes, I may even be falling in love with you. Please be careful because I don't want to explain to Jasmine how I let my intended wife get hurt."

His admission about how he felt left me speechless. What was I supposed to say? Admit how I was feeling about him right now, too? I said the first thing that came to mind.

"Your intended wife, huh?" As I said it, I slapped myself internally. I should tell him I care about him. I did want to see where this could go, but instead I was questioning what he said.

"Yes." He wrapped me in his arms before kissing my forehead. "Please be safe, regardless of how you feel about me. I needed you to know how I felt before we do this."

Before I could say anything, he turned and spoke to Tak.

"Tak, doors about open, you ready?"

Tak nodded with a gun in his hand. I hadn't dealt with guns much, but I knew their usefulness. I watched Tak jump out the almost open door to the ground and run to the hangar.

While I'd never been here, I knew the hangar was to the left of us, and the door to it was about ten feet from where we had landed.

After what seemed like an eternity but was probably about five minutes, I heard Jasper.

"Tahva, it's time. When you get find Jasmine, tell her Jasper said Chloe and Chad are fine and are nestled inside their favorite hammock."

"How will she know I actually know you?"

"Trust me, she'll know by what you tell her."

"I'll tell her. I'll be back in no time."

"I hope so. Tak will let us know when it is time to distract the guards, wait for our signal to enter the building. You can't miss it."

"Got it." I jumped out and headed toward the hangar door. Tak was right outside waiting for me.

"It's clear, Tahva, go find Jasmine."

"Did you hear anyone else in there?"

"I didn't hear anything. If there is anyone, I think our distraction will help you get in undetected once you get there."

"If not, what do you want me to do?"

"Your mission is to get Jasmine out alive."

"Thank you, Tak, for believing in me. I'll get her out."

"I know you will, Your Highness." Tak winked and ran to catch up with Markus, who was leaving the ship.

I waited next to the hangar door for Markus' signal. I was getting impatient, and about to go in when I heard loud voices and then gunshots.

Right after the gunshots, four men ran out of the hangar.

Hoping the one protecting Jasmine was one of the men who left but assuming it wasn't, I cloaked and ran inside. I took the steps two at a time and moved to the door of the office. Thankfully, it was one of those doors with a window in it, so I could see inside without giving away my entire position. I immediately saw Jasmine was tied to a chair and trying to release herself by tipping over. Hearing no other voices and seeing no one in the room with her, I went in.

I opened the door and looked around. Jasmine's eyes had been blackened, and it looked like one of her arms was bent at a weird angle. I walked to the other door in the room. Opening it slowly, I saw it led to a staircase on the other side of the office. I didn't see anyone else or any indication someone had been there recently. I didn't want to scare Jasmine, but I needed her to know I was there.

"Jasmine, I'm here to save you."

Jasmine's head whipped in my direction. Green eyes matching those of Jasper looked over me.

"Who's there?"

I realized she couldn't see me with my cloaking on, so I let it drop somewhat.

A soft gasp escaped her mouth before she hardened again. Her eyes squinted with caution.

"My name is Tahva, and I'm here with your brother to get you out."

"How am I supposed to know this isn't another trick?"

"I'm to tell you Chloe and Chad are fine and sleeping in their favorite hammock."

She visibly relaxed and let me approach. I worked quickly on the ties holding her hands.

"Can you stand?"

"Yes, I can also run."

"Perfect, we're going to go through the door, down the stairs, and out of the hangar. Jasper's ship is waiting for us."

Not knowing what was going on outside or if the men would be back, we quietly walked through the door. We made it down the stairs before we heard a man yell for us to stop.

"Go, run through the door, and don't stop until you get on Jasper's ship. Do you understand?"

Jasmine nodded and ran toward the door.

When I knew she was far enough away, I turned and cloaked again, moving up the stairs again. The man couldn't see me, giving me the opportunity to get close. When I was within striking distance, I slammed down on the hand holding the gun, knocking it away. I kneed him in the groin. Before he could recover, I whispered in his ear, "That's what you get for messing with us." I kicked him in the chest, knocking him back. Staying cloaked, I ran down the stairs, out the building, and onto the ship.

***

"Ready?" Markus asked as I grabbed a gun off the rack.

"Yup, let's go." I knew Markus' plan, and it was solid. I hoped it gave enough time for Tahva to get Jasmine out and onto the ship. When we were in position, we waited for the whistle from Tak. When we heard it, we started yelling.

"YOU TOLD ME YOU WERE GOING TO PAY ME!"

"WHY SHOULD I PAY SUCH A LAZY HUMAN?" I smiled as I yelled back at Markus.

"IF YOU DON'T PAY ME, I'M GOING TO TAKE YOUR PRETTY SHIP!"

"OVER MY DEAD BODY!"

"WELL, WHY DIDN'T YOU SAY THAT BEFORE!" Markus fired three shots in the air.

I could hear the door to the hangar open and footsteps indicating the men were coming out to see the fight. Leaning over like I'd been shot, I waited until they were closer, and swung at Markus, knocking him onto his stomach. This was a 'fight' we'd done plenty of times before, and it was well choreographed at this point. I limped away, hoping the men would take the bait, and they did. As they got closer to Markus to see if he was dead, I quickly turned my gun on them and Markus stood with his.

"Don't move, or we'll shoot."

Two of the men got on their knees with their hands up, while the other two tried to run back to the hangar.

Markus clipped one in the shoulder while I shot the other in the back, causing him to fall and stay down. The man Markus clipped made it inside the hangar. Instead of following him, we ran toward the ship, hoping we'd given the other team enough time to get Jasmine and get back to the ship. As we rounded the corner, I saw Jasmine run inside the ship with Tak standing halfway between the door and the hangar, gun at the hangar door and keeping watch.

"Did Tahva get out yet?"

"Not yet, Captain. Jasmine said one of the guys found them, and Tahva told her to run."

Frustrated she had stayed instead of going with Jasmine but also concerned for her safety, I turned to the hangar door.

"Captain, get on the ship with Markus. If need be, I'll go in, but you are to get on the ship, NOW."

This was one of the few times Tak had ever yelled at me, and all I could do was nod and do what he said. My mind was in a tailspin over what was going on in the hangar. I wanted to help Tahva, but I knew Tak was right. I needed to be on the ship with Jasmine and the rest of the crew. Markus followed me up, and Jasmine rushed us, hugging us both at once.

"Thank you so much for coming to get me. Where are the girls? Are they okay?" Jasmine frantically looked around.

"Of course we would come get you. The girls are with Cythnia on the bridge."

Jasmine glared at Markus. "You brought your mother on a rescue mission?"

"Do you think she would let me not bring her? This is my mother after all."

Jasmine and Markus walked to the door out of the loading bay. It took Markus a second to realize I wasn't coming.

"Captain, aren't you coming?"

"No, I'm going to wait until Tahva and Tak get back on board."

I heard Jasmine ask Markus how we found her and who Tahva was as they walked to the bridge. I smiled knowing she would be okay. It looks like some bumps and bruises. One of her arms looked weird, but not being a doctor, I had no idea what it meant, if anything. I knew once Botha looked her over, she would be fine. At least physically. I don't know what else they did to her I couldn't see, and it worried me.

I turned at the sound of the hangar opening but couldn't see anyone coming out. Knowing Tahva was likely cloaked, I stood still waiting for her. In a few steps, I saw her hair coming out from under the suit while she ran to the ship. Tak was jogging backwards to the ship, keeping his eyes on their surroundings.

"There's a guy... I hurt him, but I don't know if he's still following," she said breathlessly as she climbed onto the ship.

I wanted to hug her, but I also didn't want to force her into anything. Surprisingly, she stopped right in front of me and threw her arms around my neck. I hugged her back before I heard the door slam open again. Tak had hopped onto the dock door and was about to hit the button.

"Get to the bridge. Jasmine and Markus are there. Tak and I will handle this." I pushed her to the door and turned before she could argue. Running up to the ship was the man Markus had shot in the shoulder. In one hand he was holding a gun, and in the other he was holding his groin. *Way to go Tahva.* As he raised his gun, he focused on me. Before I could do anything, Tak shot the man through the chest, causing him to fall flat on his back, and hit the button closing the door.

I hit the communicator button in the bay. "Markus, we are on board and good to go."

"Yes, Captain," was his reply as I felt the ship lift-off.

I patted Tak's shoulder. "Thank you."

"You go see your sister. I'll make sure all the weapons are accounted for."

I handed him the gun he'd given me earlier and turned to the door to go to the bridge.

Entering the bridge, I saw Jasmine sitting with the girls on her lap. Botha was checking her arm while Tahva and Markus were talking off to the side.

A ping of jealously zapped through me at them talking. *Why am I feeling this way?* I thought. When they noticed me walking in, they turned to me.

"Is everyone okay?"

"Botha is taking great care of me, Brother, thank you again for coming to get me."

Botha looked at me and nodded before stepping away. "She'll be okay. Her arm is broken, but it should heal soon. I gave her something for the pain, even though she didn't want anything."

"Thank you, Botha. We are forever in your debt."

She nodded as she walked off the bridge. "I'm going to make sure Tak is okay and maybe help him with dinner if there's nothing else needed from me."

"No, you've done more than enough." I turned to Markus. "Have you let the port master know about the bodies?

"Already done. He said he'll get his people out there to clean up and to thank you personally for clearing up the hangar for him. Oh, and Tahva, he said if you ever want to see Triton, you're more than welcome to come visit, but otherwise he never heard you travelled there.

"Good, the less people who know you were there, the better."

"Jasmine, do you have any idea why you were taken?"

"I don't know for sure, but it had to do with Tahva."

***

"Me?" Everyone on the bridge looked at me.

Jasmine raised her hand before speaking. "Yes and no. What I mean by it having to do with Tahva is she was mentioned multiple times by the men who took me. But I think it was actually you, Brother, who caused me to get kidnapped."

While everyone turned to look at Jasper, I kept my eyes on Jasmine. Why would they be saying my name? Before I could say anything, Jasper spoke up.

"Why do you think it was because of me?"

"I think it's because you matched with Tahva and because of your pending marriage or whatever was going to happen. They wanted to take me to stop whatever you may have been planning to do."

"What you're saying is, it's both of our faults?"

"Yes and no. I honestly think these were hired men trying to stop you from marrying Tahva, but it wasn't either of your fault, really. I don't blame you, so please don't blame yourself. You both came and saved me, and I'm fine for the most part." Jasmine lifted her broken arm.

"I'm so sorry. If I'd known they'd come after you, I wouldn't have agreed to go to Io."

"Stop, you do what you do because of who you are, and I do what I do because of who I am. I don't want you to change because you think I may be in danger." Jasmine hugged the girls before whispering for them to go track down Tak and Botha. They giggled, jumped down from her lap, and ran out of the bridge.

"Now with the girls are gone, I can tell you more. Sit down, first."

Markus, Jasper, and I sat on the floor with Jasmine like she was going to tell us a bedtime story. Such a weird thought to have at the time, but it was fitting.

"After I was kidnapped, I kept my mouth shut and listened. Apparently, they were paid by someone to kidnap me in hopes of pulling you out of Io. Their goal was to keep me until you went looking for me and then go in and either kill or hold Tahva. They never talked specifics around me. When we got near Jupiter, they received a call, from who I assume was the payer, saying the mission had changed because the men on the ground on Io couldn't find her, and she was 'missing'. They were supposed to hold me on Triton."

"Just hold you here?"

"The plan was for you to show up. They were going to keep us both until they found the princess. They know about Jasper and Tahva's matchmaking situation and were going to use him to get her out of hiding."

"Wait, so you were near Jupiter when we left for Earth? Who knew you were coming with us?" Jasper turned toward me.

"Your crew, Marci, and the port masters. Oh, and the police and Botha." I tried to remember anyone who could have known or heard me talking.

"We know none of them had anything to do with it. Jasmine, do you know if it was a male or a female on the phone giving the orders?"

"It was definitely a male who was in charge of the men who kidnapped me. They said, 'him' multiple times when talking about him, said he had power on Io and to not make him mad."

Jasper looked at me. "While we are enroute to Europa, I don't want you to tell anyone you're on the ship. I also want you to think about any men who have 'power' who would want you dead."

"I don't know anyone with or without power who would want me dead, but I'll think about it."

"One more thing I forgot, the crew said your 'destiny would never be fulfilled' if the man paying them got his way." Jasmine shrugged at the comment.

"My destiny? They must have been talking about me becoming queen. It meant either I would be killed, or Jasper would, who is supposed to be my husband was killed, causing me to forfeit my seat since I wouldn't be married."

"Probably, but they didn't elaborate. I don't think they were smart enough to elaborate if you know what I mean. I think they were hired guns, because if they were smart, they would have taken the girls too. Leaving them to tell Cynthia immediately, not smart."

"True, but I'm glad they didn't take them. They're so sweet and innocent." I smiled as Jasmine lit up from my compliment.

"They're great, but don't let them fool you. They're more like their uncle than like me." Her eyes sparkled as she looked at Jasper who was already in a side conversation with Markus. I hadn't noticed him and Markus stand and move off to the side while Jasmine was telling her story.

"Is he always like this?" I gestured toward them.

"Ignoring me? Yup always." We laughed.

"It's probably time to get our food, or else the girls may eat everything before we get there. I've seen them eat Tak's cooking." I stood and helped Jasmine stand.

"Thank you. Yeah, their small size is deceiving; they can put it down. I'm still a little sore. Speaking of sore, where am I sleeping? This isn't a big ship." She suddenly looked at me. "Where are you sleeping?"

"I'm in the captain's quarters, but Jasper sleeps on the floor and is usually on the bridge while I'm sleeping. Then I'm on the bridge with Markus while Jasper sleeps. The spare room has Cythnia and the girls, Botha is in Tak's room while he stays in the armory. Maybe you can kick Markus out of his."

"I've known him long enough, I am definitely kicking him out of his so he can give it to his mom, and I'll sleep with the girls."

"I'll let you be the one to tell him."

As we walked and talked on our way to the kitchen, I realized this was someone I could be friends with. Like real friends, not the fake friends who want to be with me at the club. Too many people want to be my friend because they knew they would get the same treatment I do. I realized I didn't have someone who would listen to me during bad days but have fun on good days. I miss my mom the most on those bad days. She was always there for me.

As we got close to the kitchen, we could hear the laughter of the girls and smelled what could only be described as baked bread. It smelled so good, and my stomach rumbled in agreement.

CHAPTER 17

I watched Jasmine and Tahva walk out before turning back to Markus.

"Do you think this has something to do with the attempt at the club?"

"Maybe? But I think it may be more. It sounds more like they don't want her to ever become queen. They didn't just want you to be injured. I also don't know if their intent is to kill her. If she didn't marry you, she couldn't be queen, and they wouldn't have to kill her. But if they were also going after you, maybe it is about the marriage."

"Either way, we need to keep her protected. It wouldn't hurt if we could find out what was going on there as well. Can you start looking into the royal council members? I have a feeling something shady may be going on with them."

"I can put some feelers out, but I don't want to put out too many because people may get suspicious."

"I understand. Europa is looking like an even better option than Io with this new information, but we can't stay there forever."

"I say we land there, stay a couple days, see if we can find anything, and go back to Earth?"

"I can't take Tahva away from her family, especially with her father in hiding. But I don't want her to take over the moon without some answers."

"Well, and you have to marry her."

"Don't remind me."

"Captain, if I may, I've seen the way you look at her, why not marry her? Even if it isn't romantic, I think she is open enough to allow us to keep flying."

"You know my parent's history. I don't know if I want to marry someone for an arrangement. Look at Raf and Jasmine. I wouldn't want Tahva to lose me like Jasmine lost Raf."

"I understand, Captain. Remember, strong, independent, beautiful women who are your height don't come around often, and she hasn't killed you yet, so it may be a win-win."

"I agree, and I'll consider your words. In the meantime, let's eat, get everyone somewhere to sleep, and get to Europa."

"Sounds good, lead the way."

I walked toward the kitchen and the sounds of my and family. Not crew and family, just my family, every single person on this ship, even Botha, were part of my family, and it was my job to protect them.

When we got to the kitchen, it was standing room only. If I was going to have this many people on my ship frequently, I may have to reconsider getting a bigger ship.

"About time, Captain. They almost ate it all." Tak handed me a bowl of soup with a slice of bread while Botha handed Markus the same.

Even with the laughter and talking, as I ate my food, I thought about what Jasmine's captors had said about Tahva's destiny. I needed to talk to her alone about the way the Ioian government acted, and if there was anything she could add. I did not want to go back to Io without all the information I could get. That reminded me,

I would have Markus look into the history of Io while he was digging to see if there were answers for our questions about destiny.

****

Jasmine had conned, or negotiated, his room away from Markus, and we all went back to our rooms. I could hear the girls telling their mom all about Chloe and Chad and how Tak had fed them leftovers. I thought about what it would be like to have my own children. I'd never considered having kids, but now I'm destined to be queen. If I didn't create an heir, the royal line would end with me, and I don't know if I was ready for my family line to end. If you had asked me a year ago what I wanted, I would have said I couldn't care less if the royal line ended with my dad, and I lived my days partying and enjoying life, but I've changed. I haven't decided if it was a good change, but it was a change nonetheless.

I knew Jasper wanted to talk once we got back to the room, especially since Markus said he would watch the bridge. I think he was grumbling about losing his room. Let him pout. I would have to face Jasper sooner or later, why not now?

Walking into the room, I sat on the bed waiting for him to come in. When he didn't immediately, I used the bathroom and got ready for bed. I had finished brushing my hair when Jasper came in. Without saying anything, he came up and put his arms around me, kissing me lightly. I wasn't ready for much more than kissing, but it was a good start. I wrapped my arms around his neck in return and leaned into him. Jasper's hands ran up and down my back before stepping back.

Looking at him, I stepped away. "We should talk before any more of this happens." I motioned between him and I.

"I agree. I'm glad you're okay." Jasper sat on the bed, giving me enough space to sit down next to him.

I took ahold of his hands. "I'm glad you're okay as well, and we saved Jasmine before she got hurt more than she did." I sat there as he gathered his thoughts.

***

Looking down at her hands holding mine, I almost forgot what I wanted to talk to her about. It all came crashing back.

"I need to know everything about your planet's history, and how the government works. That is, if you know." I hope I didn't offend her with that statement.

"Of course I know. All I did for the first half of my life was learn about my damn moon. What do you want to know?"

"A lot of royals grow up with a set future they can't control. At least that's what happens on Earth, from what I've always been told. Was it like that on Io? Something you were told you were destined for when you were younger?"

"Other than possibly developing the same disease my mother had, and I was going to be queen when my father died or was otherwise removed, no."

"So, you were raised to believe you were destined to be the leader of the moon when your father was not able to?

"Our government is run by the king or queen. However, we have a regency council who helps us make decisions because it would be impossible for the leader to know everything all the time. Each council member has a set region and industry they look over and reports back to the leader."

"How are the council members chosen?"

"A variety of ways. They could be voted in, they could be chosen because they were a leader in a chosen industry, or they could be the child of a former council member."

I rubbed my face, trying to figure out if what she was telling me connected any dots. I looked at her as she waited for more questions.

"The moon is run by one or two people but has a committee to help them. What does the general population think of the government?"

"As far as I know, they love it. We are self-sustaining, we've reached out to start building on Europa so Ioians can move there if they choose, and we don't have a ruling class nor a lower class."

"No one who specifically would harbor any negativity toward you?"

"Not that I can think of. There are a few regency council members who had an issue with my father expanding toward Europa, but they don't get the final say. Disagreements have happened in the past, but usually they get over it fairly quickly."

That gave me an idea I wanted to expand on. "Your father had an issue with a regency council member recently. Could the council member have resorted to hurting your father to get you into power? Thinking you were more malleable than he is?"

Tahva thought before answering. "I don't think so. I know the council member my father fought with, and while he talks a big game, he doesn't have the resources to pay for someone, nor does he have the access to do it himself."

Cocking my head, I questioned her. "What do you mean by access?"

"The only way a council member could meet with the leader is at a public space, like a restaurant or at the royal house. My father told me he met the council member who he had the argument with at an approved restaurant for dinner."

"How do you keep regency councilors from meeting at other locations?"

"I don't know it all. What I do know is now they aren't able to interact with the leader outside of set locations. It's for the safety of the leader and their family, if they have one, as well as to remain transparent for the public."

Now I had questions for Markus to look into because I couldn't determine how the government could restrict movement without everyone knowing about it.

"One last question, can the council members get near you outside of the set areas?"

"As far as I know, yes. I don't know if the restrictions are for only the leader, or for their entire family. The one who would know is Roald, but he's with my father. Or maybe Marci, she may know. I can reach out to her."

"No, I don't want you reaching out to anyone right now until we have a better handle on what's going on and if you are actually a target."

"For how long? I need to check in with Marci to see if my father has contacted her."

"Do you trust her explicitly?"

"Yes, I do. She's the one who helped me with the suit, and she's always been there for me."

"Let me think about how we can reach out to her without anyone finding out about you being on my ship or where we're going."

"I'm going to bed unless you have more questions for me?"

"No, I don't think so. I'm going to see Markus at the bridge."

Without thinking, we stood at the same time. I reached out to hug her, and she sank into my chest. Going from her club days to possibly being the target of a murder plot had to be a lot for her. I held her while she sighed and stood there. After a bit she stepped back.

"Tahva, we'll figure this out. I won't let anything happen to you."

Smiling sadly, she nodded. "I hope you're right. I want to go home at some point."

"I know you do. Get some rest, and when you wake up, we'll be on Europa."

Without saying anything else, she crawled into the bed. I stood there before closing the door behind me.

My mind was whirling as I walked toward the bridge. I wonder if Markus was able to find anything out while I was talking to Tahva.

"Hey Captain, did you learn anything new?" Markus didn't turn when I entered the bridge.

"She did mention something interesting. She didn't think the regency council member who argued with her father at the restaurant had the resources to hurt him. Did you find anything about him in your research?"

Markus looked up from what he was reading. "Yes, actually. Unlike other government systems, the royal council only makes as much in pay as the average citizen of the moon, which is pretty good compared to other places. But since they only make the average, they don't have a lot of expendable income, and their income and expenses are all available to anyone looking for the information."

"That answers one question. Does this mean the royal family has a lot more money than everyone else?"

"Technically no. They make the same amount as the citizenry, but they can have wealth from previous leaders. When Tahva becomes queen, not only will she be paid, but she'll inherit all the money from previous leaders, who were all from her family, making her the richest person on the planet."

"What happens if she dies, or isn't able to take over her role as queen?"

"It gets fuzzy because it's never happened before. From what I can find, she'd lose the majority of her inheritance and have to move out of the royal house. As to who would take over, it would be a vote among the regency council. One would take over the spot of king, and their family would be given everything."

"The regency council has motivation for her father to be gone and for her not to take his seat."

"Yes and no. It would take a unanimous decision by the council as to the new leader. From what I can find, they never unanimously vote for anything."

"Not a good motive there, then. Did anything else in your research indicate who may want to hurt her?"

"No, everyone seems to think she's a party girl, but they don't think her being queen would be detrimental to the moon or its people. In fact, according to the circuit, there are a lot of younger people who are actually looking forward to having her as queen, someone closer to their age who may progress the moon more."

"So, likely no one from the public either? Does it say anything about there being a reason why the council members were not able to get near the leader except for specific places?"

"I saw something briefly mentioned. It sounds like when the council member is selected or sworn in, they're implanted with geographically set transmitters. When the regency council was formed, they were worried they would put undue pressure on the king or queen by being able to interact with them at will and outside specific parameters."

"What happens if they see the king or queen out on the town?"

"If it's for a brief amount of time, nothing will happen. For anything longer, it will give them an incapacitating headache to the point of needing medical care."

"Ouch, that seems harsh. How did that idea come about?" I'd heard of similar strange things before. I was confused by such a seemingly peaceful people suggesting something so torturous.

"Wait, they imposed this on themselves?" I assumed it was the leaders who'd imposed it.

"It appears so." Markus shrugged.

"Go get some rest, I'll watch the bridge until we get close to Europa."

"Sounds good, Captain." Markus left the bridge.

I could tell he was tired as he stumbled as he walked out the door. I knew my ship all but flew itself, so I sat and let my mind wander, hoping to connect the dots with what was happening on Io and Tahva. I didn't want to think about her and I right now, but I couldn't stop thinking about what the future might hold, if anything, for us.

CHAPTER 18

I woke to Jasper's voice coming over the speaker.

"We will be landing in twenty minutes. Please secure anything if needed."

I jumped up, not realizing I had slept as long as I did. I thought Jasper was going to wake me up. Quickly getting ready, I wanted to be able to watch as we landed on Europa. I put my hair up and put on comfortable clothes. I almost ran into Tak as I stepped out the door.

"Why are you in such a hurry, Tahva?" Tak moved a piece of bread to his mouth.

"I want to be on the bridge when we land. I've never seen Europa."

"Well, hurry up. Botha and I are going to be in the loading bay."

"Why?" I'd seen them getting closer over the time Botha had been on the ship, but I didn't understand why they didn't want to be on the bridge.

"I'm always in the bay when we land in case we need to fight someone. Botha is there this time in case there's a medical emergency."

I noticed he blushed a little when he talked about Botha.

"Well, have fun." I patted him on the shoulder before rushing to the bridge.

"Nice of you to join us." Jasper joked as I stepped onto the bridge. The moon was quickly approaching, and it was beautiful. I could see the new construction would eventually be housing and work areas for Ioians and others. The lake would be a great vacation spot for many.

My father was excited for these developments, and I hoped he lived long enough to travel to see it for himself. Of course he would, I told myself. He was going to be fine, and when we got this all figured out, we would travel there together.

"I really wanted to see the moon." I was so excited I couldn't stop bouncing on my toes.

"You'd never guess she hadn't travelled much, huh Markus?" Jasper smiled at my excitement.

"Hold on to something Tahva, because this won't be a smooth landing. They'll still building the spaceport." Even with his warning, it didn't stop me from peering through the windows as the port grew larger. There were a couple of other ships there. It looked like they were unloading supplies and workers.

Markus announced our arrival and asked to be assigned a hangar away from others because our business was going to take longer.

"Please state your business and origination."

"Earth, and we are here for a diplomatic meeting with our on-board client."

"Do you want a developed hangar with assistants, or is one under construction okay?" The port master's voice came over the speaker.

"Under construction, as long as it's quiet, would be perfect."

"Yes, the construction on this section is not scheduled to start again for a few months. Will your task be completed by then?"

"Yes, it will. Thank you. If you need anything, please communicate via the ship versus sending anyone to the hangar. Alright?"

"Yes, it is. Please let us know if you need anything else."

"Thank you, Europa port master." Markus clicked off the communicator and turned toward me and Jasper.

"We should have some time without any more questions." Markus turned and piloted the ship to the designated hangar.

The Port Master was right, the hangar was a good distance from the other two ships, and there was no one walking around it. The doors of the hangar opened as we got closer, and Markus set the ship down near the back.

"At least there's power." I joked.

"I have already pulled the schematics for the entire area. I need to know what hangar we are going to. Most of them are similar with two offices, nine rooms, and a large fully-furnished kitchen. I don't know if they're always furnished, but the port master won't have time to furnish it if it wasn't."

"I'm sure Jasmine and the girls will be excited."

"I'm sure they will be. Why don't you go tell them," Jasper suggested.

"I can do that and get some food at the same time." As I walked off the bridge, I could hear Jasper and Markus talking about what they hoped to accomplish on Europa.

***

I waited until Tahva was to the door before I turned to Markus.

"While you were sleeping, I did some more research into Io, and I can't find anything related to the council members speaking negatively about the king or wishing for a different governmental system. I listened to the circuits and read whatever I could find, but there was nothing pointing to anyone who wanted to hurt Tahva or her father. What are we missing?"

"I thought about it a lot before I fell asleep, and nothing clicked. We need to figure out how to get more information from Io or something."

"Tahva told me she believes she can trust Marci, but we need to figure out how to get in touch with her without someone intercepting the message."

"It's not like we know anyone on the planet, unless you do?" Markus was right. We didn't know anyone on Io, at least not to the point of being able to trust them with something like this.

"Wait, Botha's cousin was on Triton. Where was he heading after?"

"I don't know, let's find out." Markus called for Botha.

While we waited, I kept trying to think about what this could all lead to.

"You called, Captain?" Botha announced herself as she walked through the door.

"Your cousin was going to Triton, right? Do you know where he was going after?"

"He was dropping stuff off and heading to Io to get some local food before travelling back to Mars."

"Do you trust him completely?"

Botha didn't hesitate before answering, "With my life, Captain."

"I need you to contact him and tell him you need him to meet with someone on Io if he is still there."

"Anything else?"

"Yes, tell him more information will come separately and to make sure no one follows him to his meeting."

Botha moved to the communicator and contacted her cousin. "Yes, I'm fine, no I can't tell you more. Do I need to tell Auntie what you were doing on Triton? As I thought. Jasper will be contacting you in—"

Botha looked at me and I held up ten fingers. "Ten minutes, on—"

Markus handed her a piece of paper with the secure transponder code.

Relaying the code to her cousin, she nodded. "Yes, your secret's safe with me." Rolling her eyes, she clicked off the communicator.

"Do I even want to know?" I asked, not knowing if I did.

"Igo has a girlfriend on Triton, and his mom would be unhappy to know he seeing someone who isn't a Martian."

"Ahh, yeah. I can see how it wouldn't be something he wants his mom to know, at least not for the time being."

"Thank you, Botha."

"Captain, I would do anything for Tahva and her family."

"I know, and I feel the same way."

Botha nodded before leaving.

"Markus, what are we going to have him tell Marci?"

"I think we need to keep it short and to the point. I don't want to put her in danger, but we also need to know who may be willing to hurt Tahva."

"Simple and to the point."

The next ten minutes seemed to drag as we waited to contact Botha's cousin.

When it was time, I logged into the secure communication system and put in the code. Within one ring, I heard a man's voice.

"Is this Igo?"

"Yes, is this the Human, Captain Jasper?"

"It is. I'll make this short. It's imperative you travel to the Royal mansion pretending to be a delivery person. I need you to get a message to Marci, and only Marci. Do you understand?"

"Yeah, yeah, Marci, delivery person. What's the message?"

I looked over the communicator at a smirking Markus

"Tell her Jasper and Markus are seeking information regarding a threat to our passenger, a diplomat from Titan."

"But the princess isn't —"

"Yes, but I don't want people to know she's on board. Do you understand?"

"What if Marci asks me about her?"

"Tell her you have no knowledge of the princess, and you're just carrying a message. Do you understand?"

"Yeah, how's she supposed to get back in contact with you?"

"She's to contact you regarding a shipment to Europa."

"You tell Botha if she keeps holding this over my head, I'll tell my mom myself."

"Thank you, Igo. I'll do that." Clicking off the communicator, I looked at Markus, and we shook our heads. There was no way he would tell his mother. Martian mothers are fierce, and I wouldn't want to be on the bad side of one.

"And now we wait." Markus put up his feet.

"Yup."

Then we waited. The next week consisted of Tak cleaning and recleaning the armory and kitchen. I think even Jasmine and the girls were getting restless on Europa.

***

"Markus, here's your coffee," I announced as I walked onto the bridge. Sometimes it felt like all I did while I was on the ship was get people coffee, but it made me feel useful. I was useful on Triton, but since we brought Jasmine back onto the ship and landed on Europa, I've felt like I couldn't do anything productive.

He turned toward me with his finger to his lips telling me to be quiet.

I was about to tell him no one shushes me when his next words froze me on the spot.

"You have information about the king's death? No, I don't know where the princess is. When have I ever lied to you?" Markus looked up at me from the comm shaking his head.

On hearing of my father's death, I wanted to run out of the bridge. I wanted to run, scream, do something. But I needed to hear what else Markus said and why someone was looking for me. What was going on? My father couldn't be dead.

"What did you say?" I thought he was going to throw something.

"Seriously, if I wasn't in space right now on a job, I would be showing you how much I care about my job." He paused for a moment while listening.

"No, we're going out to the far reaches past Neptune."

Markus fisted his hand and brought it down on the desk. "Oh, you're going to tell the captain? Tell him what? If you don't stop talking right now, we're going to have words when I get back to Io."

He looked at me and smirked. "Oh, you want me to tell you where the princess is? Why do you think I'm my captain's personal assistant? Just stop now, and we'll talk when I'm done with this job."

He held up his hand mimicking someone talking. "I'll work on finding out where the princess is, but Captain is sleeping. I'm not going to wake him for some petty finder's fee to find the daughter of someone who lives on an entirely different planet, moon, whatever Io is considered."

Markus ended the call and rushed to my side.

"Tahva, breath." Markus had his hands on my shoulders when I heard the whoosh of the bridge doors.

"Why are you telling Tahva to breathe? What's going on here?"

I ran and threw my arms around Jasper. Through sniffles, I barely got out what Markus had said about my father being dead. I could feel Jasper's head rise off the top of mine to look at Markus.

"Captain, I got a call from someone on Io. I had to lie some, but supposedly Tahva's father was found dead. The caller's saying someone's looking for her, and they don't believe I don't know where she is."

Hearing Markus say my father was dead caused me to start crying again.

Jasper's arms tightened around me until the crying slowed. Gently pushing me away from him, he looked at me.

"Tahva, honey, will you go see Jasmine and the girls while I talk to Markus?"

"No, I want to be here."

"Tahva, please go now. I'll talk to you once I find out exactly what's going on." Jasper nodded at Markus before pulling me back in for a hug and kissing my forehead. "It'll be okay."

"Will it? I've lost everyone now. I have no one," I yelled at him while I walked out.

"You have us, Tahva; don't forget."

I couldn't see straight as I passed Jasmine's room. I wanted, no I needed, to hit something, to work out, to do something productive. Instead of going to see Jasmine, I turned and went toward the back of the ship.

"Tahva, are you okay?" Tak was wrapping his hands and had set up the punching bags.

"No, but I don't want to talk about it. Can you wrap my hands? I need to hit something."

I knew I could trust Tak to do it without questioning me. He seemed like the type who would let someone talk when they were ready, not forcing them.

"Yeah, come over here, and I'll get you wrapped up."

I walked over to Tak who was pulling more wrap from a bag.

For the next hour, Tak and I alternated punching the bags. It felt good to get my frustration out, and it helped clear my mind. I didn't think about Jasper and I. I didn't think about what had happened on Triton. I didn't even think about my parents, which was a first in a long time. It couldn't be true. Someone must have made a mistake. I couldn't reach out to anyone because if I did, people would know where I was. How did my life go from party girl, to rescuing someone, to having the world flipped upside down and losing my only relative. The more I thought about it, the harder I hit the bags.

The sweat was dripping down my back when Tak stopped the bag.

"Why did you stop the bag?" I was angry, sad, and confused.

"Look at your hands? They're bleeding. I'm all for beating the pulp out of a punching bag, been there myself, but you need to stop."

When I looked down at my hands, I realized even with the wraps on, my knuckles were bleeding. It was strange because I could see the blood, but I couldn't feel the pain.

As if Tak could hear my thoughts, he spoke up, "It's because you're so worked up. Once you relax, you'll feel your hands, and they'll hurt. I don't think anything's broken, but we need to get the wraps off to make sure. Do you want me to call Botha?"

Absently, I must have agreed to it because before I knew it, I was in the captain's room with fresh clothes on, and Botha was attending to my hands.

"Nothing looks broken. Are you going to tell me why you were trying to punch the stuffing out of Tak's bags?"

Shaking my head, I feared I'd start crying again. Jasper came in and asked to speak to Botha alone in the hall. It seemed like 10 minutes before Botha and Jasper came back, her eyes full of tears.

"I'm so sorry, but we'll get to the bottom of what's going on." She hugged me and left the room, leaving Jasper and I alone.

"Is it true?" I implored Jasper to tell me it wasn't true; my father wasn't dead.

"From what we can determine, there was an accident with your father's vehicle, and the burned bodies of your father and his attendant, Roald were found by a member of the regency council. However, due to the nature of the accident, there hasn't been a positive identification for either body."

"Why are they having issues with it? Our medical records, and those of the council, are accessible in the event of an accident."

"Oddly enough, your father's and his attendant's records are both missing."

"Missing? How?" This is all strange. I knew exactly where the medical records were kept. The records were inaccessible unless there was a medical need for them. They built the failsafe that if there was an accident, a council member could access them for the medical professionals.

"I don't know. However, I need you to come to the bridge and listen to the voice of the individual who called Markus asking about you."

"I can, but what good will it do?"

"We're trying to figure out if it's someone who has a legitimate need for you to come back to Io or if it could be for a more nefarious reason."

Hearing him say there was someone who may want me to return so they could possibly hurt me made it all real. All the adrenaline I had while I was using the punching bags disappeared, and I started crying.

Jasper pulled me close to him and held me while I cried. I don't remember if I cried this much when my mother died. I had an empty feeling about having no family, no one left who truly cared for me. That wasn't entirely true. I knew Marci, Roald, and everyone on the Stellar Kiwi. cared for me, but it wasn't the same as having someone flesh and blood care about you. I could almost count on one hand how many people cared about me. If that wasn't sad, I didn't know what was.

"I'm sorry. Is there anything I can do?" Jasper spoke into my hair.

Through my sniffles, I shook my head. Taking a deep breath, I looked up and kissed him. "Just being here for me is enough. Let me wash my face. We can go to the bridge, and I can listen to the voice."

"You don't have to do anything right now, it can wait." Jasper tried to push me back onto the bed to make me sit.

"No, I want to find out who did this and nail them to a wall."

Without saying anything, he stood and leaned against the door jamb while I got ready. I washed my face and braided my hair before turning to him.

"Let's go." I took his hand, and we walked to the bridge together. It was nice holding hands with him and feeling a connection.

Markus rushed toward us as we walked in. "Tahva, is there anything I can do?"

"Yes, let me listen to the individual who called you so I can figure out who did this."

I could see Markus looking at Jasper as if asking if I was okay.

"Markus, I'll be fine. I need to focus on what I can do, not what I can't." I let the rest of the sentence go unspoken.

"We record every communication coming in or out of the ship unless it's by secure communicator. When he called on the regular line, it was recorded. Are you sure you want to hear it?"

"No, but I need to."

Markus started the recording over the speaker. It was weird now hearing both sides of the conversation I'd just listened to. I closed my eyes in hopes of being able to connect the sound, and I realized why I couldn't.

"He's using a voice changer. There's articulation which may help me tell who it is. The voice sounds like no one I know. Let me listen to it again but with headphones on this time, please."

Markus looked at Jasper who nodded. He gave me the headphones and showed me how to run the recorder. I could hear Markus and Jasper talking, but I mostly ignored what they were saying, hoping to be able to determine who the man speaking was. I tried to piece together who it could be, but even the words used seemed different than anyone who was in my life frequently. Finally, after listening to the entire conversation five times, I took off the headphones.

"I believe he's Ioian due to some of the words he used, but it isn't someone who was around us, at least not often enough for us to recall them. With how many people come in and out during the course of a week, it could be pretty much anyone. I wish I could do more." I shrugged as I stood, not knowing what else to do.

Jasper walked closer and put his arm over my shoulder. "Let's get some food. Eating may help you remember. In separate news, Marci reached out to Botha's cousin, Igo, and agreed to meet up with him later about a delivery to Europa, so we may be able to get more information.

"Food sounds good, and can you please be the one to talk to Marci? I don't know what to say. What if she doesn't know about my father yet?"

"We'll cross that bridge later if we need to." Jasper casually pushed me toward the bridge doors and the kitchen when I heard Markus speaking to someone on the communicator.

"I don't care what it takes; I need those answers."

I looked up at Jasper who smiled and continued leading me toward the kitchen. I wanted to ask him what Markus meant, but I was so hungry and tired, I couldn't think straight.

When we entered the kitchen, Tak was ready with a cup of Ioian tea, a bowl of soup, and his homemade bread for me. I don't know how he knew what I needed, but it felt good while I ate. My eyelids felt heavy I thought I was going to fall asleep in the soup. Jasper nudged me and told me it was time to go to bed. I don't remember walking back to the room, but I remember him putting the blankets on me.

"Will you lay here with me, at least for a little bit?" I felt like a little girl afraid of the dark. Jasper smiled and laid down, putting his arms around me. In no time, I was fast asleep.

***

I laid there listening to Tahva as her breathing slowed, and I could tell she was finally asleep. I was worried about her. I know what it was like to lose a parent, both in fact. However, Jasmine and I had each other, while Tahva had no one. All she had Marci and her previous security guard, what was his name? Roald or something? And he had left with her father. The line of thinking caused my brain to start going through what we knew, and suddenly my brain clicked. I gently pulled my arms out from around Tahva before I walked out of the room and ran to the bridge.

"Markus, has Marci contacted us yet?"

"No, it should be soon, though. How's Tahva?"

"She's finally asleep. When Igo contacts you with Marci, I need you to ask what vehicle Tahva's father left in, if she knows. After that, I need you to contact the space police. See if they have any information on what vehicle the king was found in."

"What are you thinking, Captain?"

"I'm wondering if the body found was actually the king, or if it was someone else."

"You think the king faked his own death?"

"I don't know, but there's something bugging me. Remember when Tahva said their medical records are kept in a secure location in case something like this were to happen? Why haven't they been able to determine it was him? What if the person was lying to us about it, just to find out if we knew where Tahva was? I don't want Tahva to know what we're thinking until we can get more information. I think we might need to go back to Io sooner rather than later."

Before Markus could reply, the communicator went off.

"Markus here, how may I help you?"

We didn't know what was going to be said, or who was on the other side, so Markus didn't have it on speaker, and I could only hear his side.

"Marci, I assume Igo is there with you?" Markus said.

"Yes, Jasmine and the girls are okay. Everything's working out as planned."

Markus nodded to himself. "We were contacted regarding your princess. It was someone inquiring about where she was and to give us some bad news."

"So, you've heard? What do you think?"

This pause was longer, and I caught myself pacing.

"Uh huh, Jasper would like to know if they've told you what vehicle they found and who they believe was with him."

"Yes, we'll be coming back soon. Can you be prepared? We have nine including our passenger."

There was another long pause, and Markus looked at me and rolled his eyes before smiling.

"No Marci, it wouldn't be a good idea right now. Maybe after we figure out what's going on. Thank you, Marci, and please be safe." Markus clicked off the communicator before turning to me.

"Stop. Before you ask anything, let me tell you what I learned from Marci and Igo."

As much as I wanted to tell him to shut it and to let me speak, I knew I needed to hear him out first. "Marci said she did know about the supposed death of the King Xi and Roald, who was with him at the time. I guess the regency council is all in a tizzy trying to determine where Tahva is because she needs to take over the throne. She did ask about you, Jasper and Tahva, but since you heard my side, you know I didn't say anything."

"Anything else?" I needed more information than Markus was giving to decide.

"She said she hasn't heard of anyone who was aggressively looking for Tahva or who would risk her health. All the regency council were concerned, but they could rule for a week or two if needed before she returned. There's currently nothing happening needing a king or queen to attend to. She did mention one council member complaining about shipping stuff to Europa, but it was in passing, and it wasn't something the council took up."

"So, she hasn't seen or heard anything that would cause her to worry about us returning with Tahva?"

"No, she's excited about everyone coming and requested we provide additional security as needed since she's currently the ranking member of the mansion. She did want to know if we wanted a welcome home gala for Tahva, which I told her wasn't a good idea. Other than security, everything else seems normal."

"Back to Io we go. Keep your eye out. Let's get about 8 hours of sleep for everyone, and then we lift-off. Can you make sure to call everyone to the loading bay before we leave? I want to talk to everyone."

"Are you going to be sleeping?"

"Yes, and you need to as well. I want us to be refreshed and prepared for what we could be dealing with on Io."

"Will do, Captain." He shut down the bridge and went with me back to the rooms.

"Wait, where have you been sleeping since your mother took over your room?"

"On the floor. It isn't too bad when you get used to it."

I laughed as Markus went into his room, and I continued to mine. Well, I guess it wasn't mine anymore; it was our room.

Entering the room as quietly as I could, I laid on the bed. I couldn't stop thinking about what we would or wouldn't find on Io, and how it could affect Tahva. In the back of my mind, I wondered if we needed to get married sooner than we planned for her to take over the throne, especially if her father was dead.

As I laid there, I heard her cry out. I rolled onto my side and wrapped my arms around her. She burrowed into me and her body calmed. While I wish she wasn't dealing with this stuff, it made me feel good knowing I was able to be there for her.

I woke with a start as Markus' voice came over the speaker, asking for everyone to go to the loading bay for a meeting. I looked down and Tahva was in the same position she had fallen asleep in, with her body up against mine, and my arms wrapped around her.

I knew she was strong and independent, but so was Jasmine. When Raf died, she still needed someone to be there for her. I wish I could've stayed longer, but every time she looked at me, I felt she wasn't seeing me, the brother, but the man who told her that her husband was dead. I couldn't see her face so devastated every day, and so I decided to selfishly leave.

I gently woke Tahva to let her know we were going to have a meeting in the loading bay. She looked so tired but got up and ready while I went toward the kitchen. I wasn't hungry, but a cup of coffee for me and tea for Tahva would be perfect. Tak and Botha were already there. When I walked in, Tak placed a cup in front of me on the table along with a plate of food.

"You didn't have to cook; the coffee's enough."

"Captain, you need to eat, and I have a plate for Tahva when she gets up, too."

"You have what for me, Tak?" I smiled at her as she walked in. I couldn't help but smile in her presence.

"I have breakfast for you for before we have our meeting."

"Tak, you shouldn't have, but I really appreciate it."

"You're more than welcome. We'll leave you two in here to eat while we go to the loading bay."

"Sounds good, Tak. Thanks again for the food."

"Anytime, Captain." Tak and Botha walked out, leaving Tahva and me.

"Tahva, I need to talk to you about something."

She looked up from her food and waited for me to continue.

"Markus was contacted by Marci yesterday. We're going back to Io. I wanted to tell you before I told everyone else at the meeting we're about to have."

"Does she know about my father? Does she know who contacted you about me?"

"Yes, she does, and no, she doesn't. She said the council's looking for you, but they aren't being aggressive about it. They aren't changing anything."

"Why are we going back?"

"Because I think whoever is looking for you won't stop until you are found, so why not go back to Io and get them to come to you versus us running?

CHAPTER 19

He was asking me to put myself out there in hopes of getting whoever was looking for me to come out into the open. It was scary, but I was also tired. I wanted to be home, I wanted to continue living my life, and I wanted Jasper in my life.

"I want to, but I'm scared."

Jasper reached over and took my hand. "What are you scared of?"

"I'm scared of you or the rest of the crew getting hurt. What happens if something happens to Jasmine or the girls?"

"Tahva, the crew and I won't allow anything to happen to you or to anyone else on this ship. Don't worry about Jasmine, she's fierce when provoked, and she'll protect her girls. I wouldn't want to be in a fight against her. Please don't worry about us. Let me do it, okay?"

I looked at him and saw the sincerity in his face. He would protect me, I knew he would. It wasn't just words for him, it was so much more. It was then I realized I needed him with me. It wasn't a want; I needed him in my life. How this would look once we landed on Io, I didn't know, but I needed Jasper in my life.

"Are you ready to go to the meeting?" I asked.

"Yes, I'm almost done with my food, and we can go when I'm finished." Jasper smiled as he continued to eat.

When Jasper was done with his food, we walked hand in hand to the loading bay. By the time we got there, everyone else was already there, including Jannie and Juju, standing near Jasmine.

"This'll be quick, but I wanted to let you all know we're going back to Io. We'll be going directly to the royal mansion. Later, Tahva and I may go out so people can see us, but Jasmine, you and the girls will stay at the house with Marci and Markus, at least initially. Do you understand?"

"Yes, always the protective brother." Jasmine rolled her eyes.

The rest of the crew chuckled as she said it. It was true, and I wasn't ashamed.

"Damn straight, and I will always protect you. We're going to figure out what's going on, and probably have a circuit conference to announce her taking over the throne."

No one said anything so Jasper continued.

"At this point, I anticipate us being there for a week, two at the most. Markus, I want you to put out feelers for jobs. No exact timetables, but I want people to know we'll be back on the scene soon."

I didn't know Jasper and the crew were planning to leave so soon, and I tightened my grip on his hand. How did I tell him I wanted him to stay without sounding needy? Maybe I needed to have a conversation with him. He looked over at me but didn't say anything. Maybe he didn't care about me the same way I cared about him. It wasn't something I wanted to think about right now with everything going on.

"If there's nothing else, we'll lift-off in 30 minutes. Tahva, do you have anything to add?"

"Yes, please. I'd like to explain what happens with a member of the royal family dies." I wanted to talk to him about more, but this was a way to ease him into the conversation.

"Sounds good. If anyone needs me, I'll be in our bedroom. Oh, and girls, make sure Chloe and Chad are secure when we lift-off. I don't want them to get hurt."

Jannie and Juju nodded as they ran off to their room. The rest of the crew left the bay.

I heard Jasper say, 'let's go to our room'. It caused little butterflies in my stomach. I was falling for this man. I hoped it wasn't one sided.

Jasper held my hand as we walked toward the room. As we walked in, he sat. "I think we should sit on the bed versus standing for this type of conversation."

I nodded and sat beside him. Turning to face him, I felt it was now or never.

"Don't speak until I say what I need to, okay?"

Jasper nodded.

"I like you, and I want you in my life. I don't know what it'll look like, but I want to at least give us a try. When you asked Markus to start looking for jobs, I got scared you were leaving, and I wouldn't be able to take the throne. We wouldn't get married, and with my dad dying, I won't have anyone. I don't want you to stay just because I will be alone, but I am scared."

Instead of answering me, Jasper embraced me and hugged me tightly, kissing my forehead. Eventually, he let go and sat back. He looked at me before he spoke.

"Tahva, I like you too. I wanted Markus to reach out to people for two reasons. It would give the appearance we weren't staying long, so if someone wanted to do something, it would speed up their timetable. Even if I do continue to take missions, it doesn't mean I don't want you in my life. You need to understand space is my home. It has been a long time, and while I will have places on the ground to rest, I spend most of my life in space. I want you in my life, but I need you to understand this part of me."

Jasper admitting he liked me as well made me giddy. It took all I had to listen to the rest of what he was saying, and it made sense.

"Makes sense. We'll play it day by day; how does that sound?"

"It's a plan. Now get ready to meet your fate, Princess." Jasper stood. "I'm going to the bridge. If you need anything, I'll be there."

"Thank you, and let's hope everything goes smoothly." I stood and kissed Jasper on the cheek. "Thank you for everything."

Jasper smiled before walking out, seemingly happier than I'd seen him in the time I'd known him so far.

***

"Any more news?" I asked Markus as I stepped onto the bridge.

"Some chatter about us looking for work and some about the whereabouts of Tahva, but not much else."

"Well, let's try to get back to the mansion without people seeing Tahva. I don't want the wrong people to notice if we can avoid it, at least not until she's ready."

"I'll call Igo and have Marci send a vehicle for all of us."

"Sound good, have you already alerted the Port Master?"

"Yes, but not as to who was on the ship, just how many."

215

"Have you let Tak and Botha know we may have unwanted company?"

"Yes and they are ready."

"Alrighty then, let's go."

The trip from Europa to Io took only a couple of hours, and it was still light outside when we arrived. As we landed, Tak and Botha were the first out of the ship to make sure there was no unwanted welcoming committee. Seeing nothing, Botha contacted Igo, who was driving the transport vehicle Marci had arranged for us. It was a large vehicle with tinted windows. It fit up to twelve people and had six doors. Once Tak gave the all clear, I had Jasmine, the girls, Cynthia, Botha, and Tahva all walk to the vehicle together. Tahva was in the middle. To anyone watching, they wouldn't have immediately recognized her thanks to the size of the group.

Markus and I followed Tak as the last to get into the vehicle. The whole process was short, and we didn't see anyone paying us any extra attention.

The ride to the mansion was relatively short, but I know for Tahva it must have felt much longer. She held my hand the entire way, not looking out the windows.

When we pulled up to the front door, no one was there to greet us, which initially worried me. I had Markus go to the door first to make sure Marci was there and not anyone else. As he climbed the steps, Marci ran out and toward the vehicle.

"Is there anyone else here?"

"No, I was getting the rooms ready, and I let the chef take the day off since we aren't expecting company."

Tak was next out of the vehicle. He scouted the surroundings before indicating it was safe to enter.

I ushered everyone into the house except for Marci, Markus, Igo, and Botha.

Marci made a point to hug everyone, including Jasmine and the girls, as they walked into the house. To an outsider it would appear Marci was having friends or family visit.

"I think I should stay out here, Captain."

"Tak, I need you to go inside and make sure everything is quiet."

While he grumbled, he did as I asked.

"Thank you, Igo, for driving us. I'll make sure you're compensated for your assistance." I shook Igo's hand before he went over to Botha to speak to her.

"Marci, thank you for doing all this. I want you to let the regency council know Tahva is back home, and she'll be scheduling a circuit conference soon."

Marci looked worried before lowering her voice. "Do you think she's ready?"

"No, but this needs to be done quickly so we can get to whoever is controlling this. The sooner the better."

"I'll make sure it happens."

"Thank you, and please coordinate with Markus and Tak regarding security and anything else you may need." I turned away from Marci as she went into the house to start the plans for tomorrow. "Marci, one last thing, do you know who I could speak to about the accident which supposedly killed the king?"

Her eyebrows went up a little at the 'supposedly', but she kept quiet as she thought about it. "It would be either the king's security or the moon's police. I don't know all the specifics, but it wasn't the king's personal security. The head of the moon police is named Athan, and she'll be more than willing to help. Tell her you're the head of security for the princess and give her this."

Marci reached into her pocket and pulled out a letter with the royal stamp on it.

"I figured you would want to speak to her, so I went ahead and drafted a letter giving you all the rights and privileges afforded to royal security. While you go to the police station, I'm going inside to speak to the princess. Do you need anything else from me?"

"No, this is perfect. Thank you, Marci."

She handed me the letter before turning and jogging up the steps. I looked at Markus who nodded.

Igo and Botha were speaking quietly as we approached them.

"Igo, if it wouldn't be an additional imposition, would it be possible to drive Markus and I to the Moon's main police station? Botha, are you planning to go back home with Igo, or did you want to stay?"

"We were talking about it, actually. I would like to stay until everything's been figured out. This family means a lot to me, and if I can help the princess through the death of her father, I would feel better."

"You are absolutely welcome to stay. Igo, are you needed for another mission, or do you have some time off as well?"

"Actually, I'm in between missions, and so right now, I can do whatever's needed. As long as Botha keeps her mouth shut in front of my mother, that is." Igo glared at Botha.

"Perfect. Botha, please stay while Markus, myself, and Igo go to the head of police."

"I'll get settled in, thank you." Botha turned to go up the stairs as we walked back to the vehicle.

***

The ride to the head of police wasn't long, shorter than going to the port where our ship was. As Markus and I walked in, Igo chose to stay in the vehicle. A hushed silence came over the room. I don't know if it was because we were Human or what, but everyone parted as we approached the front desk.

"Hello, we're here to see the head of police. I have this letter." I tried to hand the letter to the Ioian sitting behind the desk, but they waved me off.

"She's expecting you."

I looked at Markus who raised his eyebrows. I shrugged as I followed the Ioian to the back office. It was a large room with a desk and two chairs. A window overlooked a garden. One wall had a bookcase full of books while the other wall was full of plaques and awards. It looked like the head of police had been there for quite a while, which could be a good or a bad thing.

A thin Ioian stood from behind the desk. "Hello, I'm Athan, the head of police. I assume you are Captain Jasper Moriarty and Markus, his pilot?" She reached out to shake our hands.

"Yes, you are correct, but how and why were you expecting us?"

"Please sit, and don't be alarmed. My father, the previous head of police, went to school with Tahva's father. Their friendship isn't a secret, but also isn't widely known. After my father retired almost 30 years ago, I took over, and he moved near the lake with my mother. I've been keeping track of your movements since you first came to the moon. Actually, Roald was the one who alerted me to the situation regarding the princess needing to be married and matching with a Human."

"But how did you know we were going to come see you?"

"Before we speak, let me shut this door." Athan closed the door and flipped a light switch. "What I'm about to tell you is not to leave this room, not even to tell Tahva. Do you understand?"

There wasn't much we could do other than listen, so Markus and I nodded.

Athan sat and pulled a file from the top drawer of her desk. She handing it to me, and I opened it to see an image of a vehicle at the bottom of a cliff, completely engulfed in flames. The next images were of the same vehicle after the flames were put out. The final image was of the two bodies, one in the front seat, and one in the back. I handed the file to Markus while Athan explained what we were looking at.

"As you know, the king's life was in danger, and he went into hiding with Roald. He's a man who'd been with the family for almost all of Tahva's life, if not her entire life.

Four days ago, we received an anonymous report of a vehicle on fire near the lake. When we got there, the vehicle was totally consumed by fire. It took an hour for the flames to die down enough for the crew to work on it. Once the fire was out, we were able to determine there were two bodies inside."

"Were you able to determine who the bodies belonged to?" Markus handed the file back to Athan.

"Officially no. The report states the bodies were burned so badly we were unable to extract any useful information from them. Due to it being the king's official vehicle, we assumed that at least one of the bodies was that of the king. Unofficially, we were able to identify the one in the front. It's a man by the name of Tovak."

I raised my hand. "Wait, did you say Tovak? Is he a Martian?"

Athan looked between us before responding, "Yes, how did you know?"

Markus chose to answer. "Because we delivered him from Mars to Triton for an 'important meeting' prior to us coming here for the captain to meet Princess Tahva."

"Do you know this man?"

"I wouldn't say 'know' as much as he was a paying client. Yes, we delivered him to Triton. Why was he on Io, and why was he with the king?"

"Stranger and stranger," Athan muttered.

"What was that?"

"I said stranger and stranger. The only thing we could positively get from the second body was it was an Ioian, but nothing else. The king wouldn't be with a Martian, and if we know only one of the bodies was Ioian, then we have at least one missing person, either Roald, the king, or both. At this point, we're wondering if the presumptive report of the king's death is even true."

"We're not equipped to help you with identification," Markus replied before standing up.

I looked at him, wondering why he was in such a hurry to get out of the office.

"Yes, I know. Do you know anything which could possibly help us?"

Putting his hands on the back of the chair, Markus relayed the information regarding the communication demanding to know where the princess was. He left out the part where the caller knew the king was dead, which I found curious. Markus usually had a great memory, so either he forgot or something else was going on.

"What's the plan?" Athan asked as she stood and flipped off the switch.

"She decided to schedule it tomorrow at 10, Princes Tahva will be having a circuit conference announcing her father's death and her rightful place as queen."

"Who will be doing security?"

"My crew and I will be inside. If you can spare some officers to watch the outside, I believe it would be useful, especially since I assume you plan on attending?" I still didn't know what Markus' issue was, but I felt being polite would get us further than shutting her out.

"Yes, I'll be there, and I can have five officers work the exterior, checking credentials."

I stood and shook her hand. "Thank you, and I look forward to seeing you tomorrow."

Markus and I didn't say anything as we walked out of the station. Igo was waiting for us as we came out, and I made sure the door was shut before I turned to Markus.

"What going on? You seemed like you couldn't get out of there fast enough. Was it Athan?"

"No, not at all. It was something I saw in the picture of the second body and something she said made a thought click."

"Well, are you going to tell me?"

"I need to speak to Marci, but I have a feeling I know who did all this."

"Great, keep your captain in suspense."

"You know it isn't like I don't want to tell you. I don't want to say anything and get anyone's hopes up if I'm wrong."

"Then I'll trust you like always, but if there's something I need to know, you'll tell me, right?"

"You'll be the first."

"Then let's get ready for tomorrow."

I looked out the window as we drove back to the mansion. I couldn't believe tomorrow the party going princess I couldn't stand not too long ago would be taking over the throne of a moon. Not only was she to be queen, but she was now someone I had feelings for. I knew what I needed to do, but it was also terrifying. Apparently, Markus wasn't the only one needing to talk to Marci.

***

I woke up in my own bed, not immediately remembering we were back on Io. I sat up wondering if everything happening recently was all a dream. My father hadn't died, I wasn't falling in love with a Human, and I was still the party girl I'd always been. Maybe it wasn't a dream but a long nightmare. I'd almost convinced myself until Marci came in with food to let me know the conference was set at 10, and I needed to get ready.

"I'm sorry I fell asleep so fast yesterday. Did everyone get settled in?" I needed to start playing the role of queen, which meant worrying about other people.

"Yes. Everyone is settled in, and Markus and Jasper spoke to the head of police to square away some things for today's conference."

"I guess I better start getting ready. Can you please have the jewels delivered by 9 along with my dress?"

"Of course, Princess." Marci had a smirk the entire time I spoke to her, but I didn't think to ask her why. It was like she had a secret only she knew.

I took a shower and started on my makeup when Marci came into the room with a long, dark blue dress and a box. I knew in the box was the jewelry my mother had worn and had been held for me specifically for this day. A single tear fell down my cheek as I thought about the fact neither my mother nor father would see me crowned. Technically, I wouldn't officially be crowned until I married, but I would take over the responsibilities today.

Marci came over quietly and started working on my hair. Instead of my normal plaits, she rolled my hair into a crown. Looking in the mirror, I saw my mother looking back. I was ready for this, but at the same time, I wasn't. Time waits for no one, and soon it was time to get dressed and head down to the royal office.

Marci opened the door, and Jasper was standing there in a dark blue suit. He looked so good it took my breath away. As I came closer, he held out his hand for me. I placed my hand into his, and he turned to lead us down the hall toward the stairs. Before we reached the top of the stairs, he stopped and faced me.

"You are the most beautiful woman I've ever seen." He kissed my forehead before turning back to walk down the stairs.

As we reached the bottom of the stairs, I could see how many people there were. The royal office was overflowing, with Markus and Tak holding reporters back. As I entered the office, I saw Jasmine, Cythnia, and the girls in dresses along the wall. I'm sure Marci made it happen. Along the other wall were the regency council members. They were all there, and they all had the same facial expression of relief mixed with pride.

The conference began as most do, with the regency council calling the conference to order and each member speaking their piece. It was facetime for them to talk about their projects or what they were doing to help their specific sections. I sat and listened while they spoke, trying not to look at Jasper who was standing next to my right shoulder. I let my mind wander about how many times I'd sat through these conferences, and how from now on, I should actually pay attention. I was brought back to the present by everyone clapping and the imagers clicking. The council all came encircled me, making sure Jasper was still close but not in the image and asked me to stand.

"By the power vested in us as the regency council, we declare to all those on Io and in the solar system Princess Tahva Xi of Io is now Temporary Queen Tahva Xi of Io, where full control of royalty will occur as soon as she is married."

Each regency council member came up to my left side to shake my hand and place their palm on my forehead. As the last one approached, I heard a scuffle outside.

Everything stopped as an explosion ripped through the front of the house.

All I could hear was screaming and Jasper telling me to get down. My first thought was Jasmine and the girls, so I looked over long enough to see Markus get them down before he focused on the door.

"Jasper, the last council member, Zan—I have to get approved by him." All I could think about was my people but without getting the blessing of the final council member, I wouldn't be able to assign anyone or anything. I was helpless, and I hated it.

"I'll find him. You stay here with the others, and no matter what, do not leave. Do you understand me?"

"Yes." I hated this feeling. I wanted to be out there helping. What if people were injured? Was this my fault? Maybe I should have stayed away. Before I could think, I heard Jasper yelling.

I looked out from behind the desk and saw Jasper standing with his back to me talking to someone. In that moment, I realized I wasn't going to let things happen to me anymore. I was going to be an active participant in my life. I stood to see who Jasper was talking to.

"Roald? What are you doing here? Where's my father? Why do you have a gun to Zan's head? What's going on?" I yelled over the panicked people and orders from police I could hear.

"Oh, the rich party girl wants answers now? You didn't want answers when I tried to teach you."

"What are you talking about?" Even though Jasper was trying to keep me behind him, I stepped out from behind him to face Roald.

"You had everything, you spoiled brat. You were given the keys to the literal kingdom by your father, and you don't deserve them. When I kill Zan, your dream is dead, just like your father's. And you will be soon, too."

"How is my father dead but you aren't? You're supposed to protect him. I demand you tell me what's going on." I stood tall against the man who had helped raise me. I saw Markus coming in behind Roald and knew I needed to keep him talking.

"The princess demands, does she? You don't know anything. You took everything for granted, even me. I had been here day in and day out, and you chose to marry a Human. I was royalty!" Roald yelled at the room.

"You're my father's age, and you wanted me to marry you?" Now I was mad. Who did he think he was to tell me what I should or shouldn't do? The pieces were fitting into place, and the more pieces fitting together, the more upset I got. "You hurt my father, you threatened Jasper, and for what? In hopes I would marry you?"

I could tell Roald was getting tired of holding the gun as his arm was starting to waver. Before Markus could get to him though, I wanted to make him pay.

"What do you mean, you're royalty? Aren't you from a family of servants?"

Roald was taken back by my comment, his arm wavering more. "I'm part of your mother's extended family. I am of royal blood. When I was born, I was destined to marry a princess. When your parents only had a single daughter, I knew my destiny was going to be fulfilled, so I got a job working as your security. Being close to you, I figured eventually you would see me and want to be with me, but no. You continued to date worthless men, partying your nights away without a care in the world. I had to force you to think about your future."

Just as Markus went for the arm holding the gun, I walked up to Roald, knowing Jasper and Markus would keep me safe.

The council member who had stayed quiet through this widened his eyes and shook his head as I came closer.

"Jasper is more of an Ioian and man than you ever were. I never would have seen you as anything other than a servant." I stood, almost touching Zan. "And Roald, for your information, I am your queen, but you will never be anything to me." I shook the hand of the council member, and he touched my forehead as Markus grabbed Roald. The council member fell into me as Jasper caught us both.

Tak walked in with Athan, who arrested Roald on multiple counts.

"Wait, before you take him away, I want one thing."

Athan looked at me before nodding.

"I want all the reporters to come back in. It's safe now."

Athan clicked her communicator to let everyone know it was safe to come back in, which everyone did, all vying for the best spot.

"With everyone here, I was blessed by the final council member, so I am officially your temporary queen. Also, I would like everyone to know Roald here is the one who masterminded this whole thing. He's the one who killed my father and caused the accidents. All to marry me."

"Um, Queen, can I have a word?" Athan spoke up.

"Yes, Athan?"

"Roald didn't kill your father. Your father's at the lake house with my father and should be returning soon."

I collapsed when I heard Athan say those words.

Jasper caught me right before I hit the ground.

If I hadn't been so emotional, I'd have seen the look on Roald's face when he realized his entire plan had been destroyed.

Jasper told me later it was like poetry, something of beauty. I'm sure it was captured by an imager or two.

A hush fell over the crowd before a round of applause could be heard coming from outside. The sound continued into the house until it was outside the office doors. There was some light pushing from the reporters trying to get the best image angles as my father, the now previous king, entered the room. I ran to him and hugged him. I will never take him for granted again.

"Queen, I think someone has something to ask you," my father whispered into my ear before turning me to face Jasper.

Jasper stood there with a box in his hands. "Tahva, Queen of Io, will you allow me to make your queen status permanent by becoming my wife?" He opened the small box, which held my mother's royal ring. It was the same one my father had given my mother when he proposed.

I cried as I nodded and rushed into Jasper's arms. I could hear the imagers clicking and the reporters trying to ask questions, but all I could hear and see was Jasper hugging me and telling me how much he loved me.

"I love you, Captain Jasper Moriarty."

CHAPTER 20

6 Months later

The phone ringing out in the reception area caused me to look up from my paperwork.

"Meta, can you please get the phone."

It kept ringing so I stood and marched out there. The room was empty, and the front door was wide open. I noticed what appeared to be drag marks going out the front door but couldn't be sure. Looking to make sure no one was still there with me, I closed the door and answered the phone.

"Matching Galaxies, where we provide you a match made in space." *Gods I hated the tag line, especially with what we do behind the scenes.* "Fareh speaking."

"Fareh, this is Sith from Earth. Is this line safe?"

"I'm not sure, Sith. My receptionist seems to have left or been taken. Can I call you on your personal line?"

"Absolutely and time is of the essence."

I rolled my eyes. Sith was prone to doomsday predictions, and everything was an emergency.

Walking back into my office, I closed the door and tapped on the wall. A small panel opened, and I put in my code. A whooshing sound could be heard. When the button turned green, I knew my office was soundproof. Sitting down, I opened the bottom drawer of my desk and picked up the intercell. I took a deep breath before dialing the number.

"Fareh, thank you for calling me back so quickly. Khai has been taken." I could hear Sith's panicked voice as if she was sitting next to me.

"Sith, this has happened before. It's part of why we don't let them into the inner circle. We maintain the business front, and the receptionists don't know anything about the other things."

"I know, but what if this time it's 'The Time'."

"It isn't, the seer says we have more matches to do, and those matches will be successful before it's time to face 'The Time'."

"Fareh, how can you be so calm? What if our receptionists are really gone this time."

"Then we hire new ones. You knew the job when you took it. I'm not going to have this argument with you again."

"Should I call the other offices?"

I know Sith was trying to put on a brave face, but I couldn't have her stirring up the others.

"No, you file a police report if you haven't heard from Khai by this evening, and I'll get in contact with the other offices. Don't tell anyone outside of the network Khai's missing other than the police. Do you understand me?"

"Yes, I do. I may not like it, but I understand." Sith sounded resigned and I wonder how many more years she would be able to work at this job. It wasn't for the faint of heart.

"Thank you. I'll be in contact on this line, so keep it close." I disconnected the call. I rolled my neck before I opened my address book sitting in the bottom drawer. I hated having to make these calls, but as the leader of Matching Galaxies it was my responsibility to protect the offices.

"Tegarix? Yes, this is Fareh. Yes, we have a situation on Io and Earth. We'll need two new receptionists as well as the other offices alerted."

I listened while Tegarix ran through their normal diatribe about how we can't risk this and that. It was the same thing every time.

"Yes, we may have to speed up the timetable." Tegarix argued, which happened every time.

Sometimes I felt like I was in never ending circle.

"We won't speed up the timetable, but we need replacements, and we need to start searching for the next match."

"You are to start with the next match as soon as possible."

Their words caused me to sit up.

"Wait, you already have one? It usually takes years. A pilot and who? Are you sure?"

I had to move the phone away from my ear as they yelled at me. "Of course you're sure, I'm sorry for questioning you. We can start the process in motion."

Tegarix disconnected, and I sat back waiting for my computer to ding with the match. Now to make sure both voluntarily enter our office to be matched.

About Author

F.L. Journey is the pen name for two authors who have come together to write in a variety of genres they enjoy. Look for more short stories and novels in the future from them.

Follow us on Facebook, Goodreads, Bookbub, and Amazon. Look for announcements about future projects. Please review and share.

By signing up for our newsletter, you will be sent exclusive content.

Website: http://fljourneywrites.com/
Facebook: https://www.facebook.com/FLJourney

Other books by Author

As F.L. Journey

Ancient Resurgence Series

Ancient Resurgence: Daniel's Story

Ancient Resurgence

Cerberus Brothers Series

The Cobalt Warrior

The Crimson Scholar

The Jade Commander

Matching Galaxies

Princess and the Pirate

Anthologies

Illusions – "Death Awaits" – July 2024

Little Witches – "Growing up Teen Witch" – October 2024

As Flo Journey

PNW Syndicate Series

Carlina (Coming 2025)

Beatrice (Coming 2025)